James Albert Garland, New York Metropolitan Museum of
Art, John Getz

Handbook of a Collection of Chinese porcelains

James Albert Garland, New York Metropolitan Museum of Art, John Getz

Handbook of a Collection of Chinese porcelains

ISBN/EAN: 9783337824747

Printed in Europe, USA, Canada, Australia, Japan

Cover: Foto ©Andreas Hilbeck / pixelio.de

More available books at **www.hansebooks.com**

HAND-BOOK

OF A COLLECTION OF

CHINESE PORCELAINS

LOANED BY

JAMES A. GARLAND.

—

COMPILED BY JOHN GETZ.

—

PUBLISHED BY

THE METROPOLITAN MUSEUM OF ART.

1895.

PREFACE.

This Hand-book is necessarily limited in scope, and is not intended for the solution of vexed questions, nor in any way to supersede the more elaborate treatises on Chinese ceramics.

The Garland Collection now on exhibition embraces various types important and noteworthy for their colored decoration and their component paste; including, naturally, not only the beautiful, but the grotesque and curious as well. Though no attempt has been made to arrange the collection chronologically, the examples fairly cover the history of Chinese ceramic art for the periods which are held in regard to-day.

The Chinese attained their preëminence in this art centuries ago, a preëminence not surpassed by any modern advance. The colors of their ancient pieces possess greater vividness and depth; their forms, an originality and elegance of their own.

The following authors, whose perusal will reward the deeper student, have been largely used in compiling these pages:

Lettres édifiantes et curieuses, écrites des missions étrangères, published by L'Abbé de Querbeuf, Paris; last edition, 1780–1783. The letters of Père d'Entrecolles, written in 1712 and 1722, will be found in Vols. 18 and 19.

The work which affords native testimony respecting the history of Chinese porcelain, and the places at which it has been manufactured, is the Histoire et fabrication de la porcelaine chinoise, translated from the Chinese by M.

Stanislas Julien, with notes and additions by M. Alphonse Salvetat; Paris, 1856.

The leading scientific works on the nature of porcelain and its chemistry are the Traité des arts céramiques, by M. A. Brongniart, Paris, 1844; and La Porcelaine, by M. Georges Vogt, Directeur de Sèvres, a thoroughly technical work on both European and Chinese Porcelain.

Porcelaine de Chine, par M. O. Du Sartel, Paris, 1881, a work of great value, and beautifully illustrated.

Probably the latest important work is La Céramique chinoise, by M. Ernest Grandidier, Paris, 1894, whose collection is of world-wide reputation, and was recently given to the Louvre in Paris.

History of Pottery and Porcelain in the 15th, 16th, 17th and 18th centuries, by Joseph Marryat, London, 1868.

Oriental Porcelain and Pottery of the South Kensington Museum, by Augustus M. Franks, London, 1878.

Abriss der Geschichte des Porzellans und der Thongefässe, by Dr. J. G. Theodor Grässe, Dresden.

The works of M. A. Jacquemart, Paris, 1862 and 1873.

Descriptive and historical Catalogue of a Collection of Japanese and Chinese paintings in the British Museum, by Wm. Anderson, F. R. C. S.

Ancient Vases, by P. P. Thorns, London, 1851.

The Chinese Readers' Manual, by W. F. Mayers, London.

The marks on Oriental porcelain are given in the various editions of Chaffers; they are also to be found in works published by Dr. J. G. Theodor Grässe and others, and in Hopper and Phillips' Manual of Marks.

INTRODUCTION AND EARLY HISTORY.

The Chinese are conceded, by authorities generally, after all possible documentary research, to have been the first to manufacture porcelain. The question, When was this industry born? remains, however, to be finally solved. Some savants are content to assign its date to some time under the dynasty of Thang, A.D. 618–907; others to a much earlier period.

As we are dealing with porcelain as it appears in this collection, we must forbear to discuss the obscurely known primitive art, and attempt but superficially to penetrate the mystery of the history of ceramic art. "In order to know porcelain well," says a French writer on the subject, "it is necessary to look thoroughly into ceramic art in general." But this would include all sorts of objects made from crushed stone, earth or clay, and we must accordingly confine ourselves pretty closely to porcelain.

We shall attempt merely a brief outline of the history of this art, following its progress from the earliest time of which we have historical testimony. The common statement that vases of burnt clay existed in China as early as 2255 B.C., but that the art was invented under the Emperor Hoang-ti, 2698 B.C., may be taken as mythical and doubtful.

M. Stanislas Julien, in his translations from early Chinese books, concludes that porcelain was invented in the dynasty of Han (185 B.C. to 87 A.D.); appearing first in the land of Sin-P'ing, a district created by the Emperor Kao-tie. For a number of years following this period very little progress was made; however, we find that mention is made of a factory at Si-gan-fu, in the province of Chen-si, under the dynasty of We'i (A.D. 220–264), and also at Lo-yang in the province of Ho-nan, where all the vases made were destined for the Emperor's use. The Chinese authors barely refer to the fabrication of porcelain or pottery, as existing in the epoch of Tsin (265–419 A.D.). They do not mention any distinguished workman; but they state that the porcelain called Ngeou was blue, and known under the name of Tong-Ngeou-thao. In the first years of the period Tchi-te (A.D. 583), dynasty of Tchin, however, we learn of a royal decree ordering the inhabitants of Tchang-nan (afterwards called King-te-tchin) to make porcelain as tribute, for the Emperor's use. From this time on are mentioned the names of workmen and their productions. Thus Ho-tcheou, under the dynasty of Soui (A.D. 581–618), was celebrated for the manufacture of vases of a beautiful green, called "Lou-tse." The Chinese authors also speak of pieces with crackle surface, resembling the jade in color. The products of Thao-yu, of Tchang-nan (commencement of the dynasty of Thang, A.D. 618) were known as Kia-yu-Khi, i.e., vases of artificial jade; which he brought already finished to the capital, and offered as a tribute to the Emperor.

Père d'Entrecolles mentions in his translation that in the period of Wou-te (A.D. 621), Ho-tchong-thsou made porcelain with a white body called "Ho-yao" (porcelain of Ho), as brilliant as jade; and the Emperor decreed that Ho-tchong-thsou and other inhabitants of Sin-P'ing should make these vases for the use of the palace. The impression is here conveyed, for the first time, of a certain transparency, due to a kaolinic substance, more or less vitrified by complete baking. The white color that properly constitutes the quality of porcelain had not yet been seen; and it is not unlikely that the earlier product, referred to as "Thao," was only a sort of pottery made of earth and stone, enameled, but less thoroughly fired (Grandidier).

Doubt ceases, however, with the product of the Thang dynasty (A.D. 618–907); when vases are described as of a white color and of graceful form, solid and thin, and of sonorous sound. We learn that this porcelain was in great vogue, and called "Yao" to distinguish it from the former "Thao" (Du Sartel); the name signifying literally an object baked in a kiln, whether of porcelain or pottery. Mention is also made, in an early book on tea, of cups of this period, in blue, which enhanced the color of the infusion by giving it a greenish tint; and were considered superior to the earlier ones of dark yellow, which imparted to the tea a brownish tint. Another distinct reference is made to a porcelain made under Prince Tsien-Lieou (A.D. 907), called "Pi-se-yao" (porcelain of the hidden color), made at Youe'i-Tcheou, in the province of Tche-kiang, in which mention is made of an exterior blue enamel for the exclusive use of the palace, and not to be seen by the lower classes, because it was so pure and brilliant.

In the period of Hien-te (A.D. 954) the Emperor Chi-tsong gave his family name of "Tch'ai" to the hard paste porcelain, which was also termed "imperial porcelain." This Emperor issued an order that the porcelain for the palace thenceforth should be made of "the color of the sky seen between the clouds after rain." The authors say that this porcelain was "blue as the sky, brilliant as a mirror, and thin as paper, resonant as a Khing (a musical stone of jade), polished and glistening;" and it was also "distinguished for its fineness of texture and crackle." These objects were so much prized in after years that the fragments were set in gold and worn as personal ornaments, and called Tch'ai-yao, or porcelains of Tch'ai.

During the Sung dynasty (A.D. 960–1260) the manufacture of porcelain received greater development. We learn from the translations of M. Stanislas Julien that at the beginning of this dynasty (A.D. 960) there lived two brothers named Tchang, who came originally from Tch'-ou-tcheou, and were renowned as porcelain makers. The elder, named Sing-i, was considered the more clever; his porcelain was called Ko-yao (porcelain of the elder brother) to distinguish it from the productions of the younger. He used brown colored clay of fine quality, exceedingly thin, and covered it with a pale or a dark blue color. The glaze was beautifully crackled, and had the appearance of fish-roe. He also made vases of the color of rice and pale blue.

These were preferred because the enamel was of perfect purity, and had the iron color rim at the opening and at the foot.

History states that during the last years of the Sung dynasty artists tried in vain to imitate his work, but the clay they used was poor, and the color less agreeable.

The younger brother, Tchang-Sing-eul, made pieces of the same color not crackled; and his enamel had the appearance of being sprinkled with dew. Père d'Entrecolles mentions among them pieces of an olive-green color. Many of his pieces resembled very ancient specimens; and his productions also had a reputation at Tch'ou-tcheou, as porcelains of Tchang. The moon-light (*clair de lune*) color may be ascribed to this epoch.

At about this same period, as it is stated, in the village of Pe-thou, district of Siao-hien, province of Kiang-nan, lived many potters named Tseou, whose vases were thin, brilliant, of surpassing whiteness, and pure and graceful in form. Another porcelain of this period is mentioned as "Kiun-yao," made at Kiun, in the district of Yu-tcheou, province of Ho-nan. Among the different glazes named are Mei-tseu-tsing (the blue color of prune skin) and Kia-pi-pe (the violet of the skin of wild apples).

In the period of King-te (A.D. 1004–1007), under the Sungs, the Emperor ordered the four words, King-te-nien-tchi (made in the period of King-te), to be inscribed underneath on the pieces made for the use of the palace. Here appears a date-mark.

These objects were at once distinguished for the brightness of the glaze and for the material, as well as for their beautiful form. These porcelains, with imitations, circulated throughout the empire, and were generally called porcelains of King-te-tchin.

Between A.D. 1107 and 1117 a porcelain manufactory was established by the Emperor at Pien-liang, where were made the famous vases for the magistrates, termed Kouan-yao. They were thin, sometimes dark blue, sometimes pale blue, sometimes moon-white, bluish or dark green, or pale green. The upper rim was brown, and the foot the color of iron. The magistrate vases seem to have been imitated in various places, but the imitations are described as inferior to the originals.

It is also further recorded that the district of Ki-tcheou, later called Lou-ling-hien, had produced two clever artists, father and daughter, by the name of Chou. The elder, Chou-ong (the venerable Chou), produced many curiosities in porcelain, such as birds and animals; but the daughter, Chou-Kiao (La belle Chou), surpassed the father in workmanship and ornamentation. Their productions, of whatever color, sold almost as high as the porcelains of Tchang the elder. Five kilns in the district are mentioned. Their porcelain came to the market at Yong-ho, and was called Ki-tcheou-yao, but the productions of the family Chou were most highly esteemed.

When the dynasty of Sung passed to the South of China, (A.D. 1127), a magistrate or officer named Chao-tch'-ing-tchang established a small factory or kiln in the new capital, and made porcelain of a good quality, called Neï-yao (porcelain of the interior, or palace), distinguished for its brilliant color and transparent enamels. It was also called Kouan-yao (porcelain of the magistrates or government), distinguishing it from that made under the Sungs of the North.

Under the Yuen dynasty (Mongols), A.D. 1260–1367, we find one porcelain maker whose name has been preserved, P'ong-kiun-pao, who was established at Ho-tcheou, in the province of Kiang-nan. He was at first a gilder, but afterwards made very thin and white vases called Tche-yao, a name indicating a form with compressed centre. He excelled, however, in copying the ancient vases of Ting-tcheou. In the IV. Chinese Vol. of "Porcelain made at King-te-tchin" (Julien) it is said that his best copies were difficult to be distinguished from the older products. It is further stated that a tax was put upon all porcelains not made for the palace; whence the industry did not flourish, and so few names have been preserved.

We find, among the annals, mention of a porcelain called "Tch-on-fou-yao," made for the Emperor, the material employed for which was white and plastic, and ornamented with flowers, etc., modeled in the clay and enameled. Also that large vases were made in brilliant monochrome, and bowls, raised on feet, and basins, called "Ma-ti-pan." Special reference is made to the talent for painting and modeling on porcelain, developed during this period.

A kind of porcelain called "Hou-tien-yao" was made of coarse material, hard and tenacious; of a pale white color, and covered with a yellowish black glaze.

Vases also were made in the countries east and west of Tche-kiang. These had grace and elegance, like those of ancient make; but the kilns fell into disuse, and not a vestige of them remains.

The dynasty of Mings, which occupied the throne of China A.D. 1368–1648 (a period much shorter than the dynasty of Sung), gave to the manufacture of porcelain the greatest development. A number of clever workmen are named for their remarkable productions, and the kilns are noted as increasing, while there was no deterioration in the quality of the products. Antiquarians of the Celestial Empire, accordingly, search continually for specimens of the periods which were most esteemed, viz., Yong-lo, A.D. 1403–1425; Siouen-te, A.D. 1426–1435; Ching-hwa, A.D. 1465–1487; Kea-tsing, A.D. 1522–1567; Wan-li, A.D. 1573–1619.

Of the Hong-wou period (A.D. 1368–1398) little is known except that in its second year, A.D. 1369, a kiln was established at the foot of Mount Tchou-chan (King-te-tchin) whose products were called Kouan-tse, for the use of the palace, to distinguish them from those made for the people. They were made in blue, black and white; the latter the most esteemed. Here are found for the first time trustworthy details concerning the application of the glaze. It is stated that pieces were exposed to dry in the crude state for one year. Large vases decorated with dragons, and smaller vases, were called Tsing-yao (vases in blue); other vases of various colors were called Se-yao. The vases of Yong-lo, A, D. 1403–1425, seem to have been made of varying qualities. Egg-shell porcelains (Tho-taï) are mentioned, in white, with decoration. Some were thick, and engraved or painted in colors. Those most valued were cups on which were painted lions rolling a ball. The second sort had, within, a pair of birds, the symbol of love; a third, flowers. Cups are also mentioned, having a dark blue exterior decoration of flowers; also vases of a brilliant red.

The Siouen-ti period (A. D. 1426–1435) inaugurated an epoch, which the Chinese writers praise most highly. Under this Emperor they first made the beautiful dark blue, and embellished the objects with polychrome decorations. The first ceramist mentioned is Lo-he, who excelled in making coupes and vases decorated with crickets. In this period, also, are recorded two sisters by the name of Ta-sicou, who produced the same designs engraved in the paste on delicate cups and other pieces.

White vases with blue flowers were much esteemed, especially where the blue was pale, on a ground resembling orange peel. A brilliant red was also valued, which was obtained by crushing a red-colored precious stone brought from the West. A fish was sometimes moulded on the handles of small red cups, called "Tsi-hong;" tea-cups were much prized which had carefully painted flowers, or a dragon and phœnix, with the mark of the period engraved.

In the Ching-hwa period (A. D. 1465–1487) the blue color, owing to the failure of the supply, became inferior in quality, but the polychrome painting was brought to a high degree of excellence, and the paste was made firm, solid, and oily in texture.

In this period lived a distinguished artist named Kao-than-jin, who fabricated jars decorated with peonies and chickens. Another workman, named Ko-tchou, made fine cups for wine. Their numerous products served as models for later periods.

The period of Tching-te (A.D. 1506–1521) is notable for the decoration of porcelain. In this epoch the discovery of cobalt blue (Hoe'i-tsing) was made, and by command was used to decorate the Imperial porcelain. Hoe'i-tsing was crushed with hammers. The finest quality showed bright red spots; the second, silvered flakes. It was called "great blue" and "blue of the head of Buddha." This beautiful blue, of such superior quality, and costing more than its weight in gold, was brought to China from the West, through Arabia. With this material the ceramists were again able to produce a blue like that of the pieces produced under the Emperor Siouen-te, A.D. 1426–1435.

In the period of Kia-tsing (A.D. 1522–1567) decorated porcelain was characterized by the fine deep colors employed, notably cobalt blue, brilliant red, yellow, violet, and bluish-green. These were the chief components of the decoration, forming five colors on a white ground. The annals of this period mention porcelain sacrificial cups (Tan-tsien), imitating white jade; also other cups and small rouge boxes; and state that single colored glazes were used to cover porcelain, but one of the supplies failed (the red of copper). From that time on, it is recorded, the Emperor ordered the decoration of Imperial porcelain to be blue.

During this period a manufactory of porcelain was established in the province of Tche-kiang. The vases were called P'ing Kouan (pots), Kang (jars), Yong (amphoras), Pan (basins), Ouan (bowls). These, however, were considered inferior to those made at King-te-tchin.

During the period of Kea-tsing (A.D. 1522–1567) and Long-khing (A.D. 1567–1572) there was a clever workman by the name of Tsou'ï-Kong (the venerable Tsou'ï), who successfully imitated the old specimens. His pieces were considered the finest of his time.

In the period of Long-khing (A.D. 1567–1572) and Wan-li (A.D. 1573–1619) a potter from Ou-men, named Tcheou-tan-

ts'iouen, settled at Tchang-nan (King-te-tchin) and produced a great variety of objects. He was one of the most
celebrated of his time, and excelled in the imitation of
antiques. As soon as a vase left his hands, all amateurs
disputed for its possession. His imitations approached the
reality so closely that no one could tell the difference. They
did not mind paying enormous prices for a small piece.

In the period of Wan-li (a.d. 1573–1619) another distinguished ceramist, Ngeou-Kong, gave his name to the
porcelains made by him. He was born in the district of
Fhing, province of Kiang-nan. Among his vases were some
reproductions of the crackled porcelains of Tchang the elder.
Others were called "Kouan-yao," (porcelains of the magistrates). His copies of Sung specimens, and "Kiun-yao"
(porcelains of Kiun), including the clair de lune and violet
of the Sungs and others, were decorated in different
colors. The most esteemed were veined porcelains, in red
and blue enamels. Five other distinguished potters of the
period are on record.

In the period of Wan-li lived also, at Feou-liang, a man
named Hao-chi-khiou, who excelled in composing verses,
writing and painting. He retired secretly to a porcelain
factory, where he made vases of charming elegance. He
took the name of Ou-in-tao-jin (the old man who lived in
retreat). He was renowned for his bowls, decorated with
diapered clouds, and the celebrated egg-shell cups, of
delicious whiteness, which weighed only three-quarters of a
gramme. His coupes were of a lively red (cinnabar). He
also made vases called Ou, from his assumed name. They
were plain blue, like the famous "Kouan-yao" (porcelain of
the magistrates) and Ko-khi, porcelains of Tchang the elder,
but they were without crackle. He also made vases of a
purple color, in imitation of the antique porcelain made at
I-hing. His pieces bear the mark, at the foot, of Ou-in-tao-
jin (the monk Ou, who lived in retreat). During this period
the famous "Lang-yao" porcelain (the sang de boeuf of the
French) was made by a family of potters named Lang.

The trouble of the later Emperors of the Ming dynasty, who succeeded one another rapidly, and were constantly at war with the Tartars, probably caused the kilns to fall into decay and neglect. We hear, at any rate, nothing of their productions; and no dated pieces have been seen.

With the accession of the Tai-tshing, or Mantchou Tartars, a new period of activity commenced. Under the second Emperor Khang-he (A.D. 1661-1722) a great impulse was given to ceramic art; the peaceful reign of this emperor extending over sixty years. His great indulgence, and perhaps the assistance of Jesuit missionaries, led to many improvements in the manufacture of porcelain, and the introduction of several new colors.

In this period, Thang-in-siouen, director of the Imperial factory, made porcelain vases with oily clay. They were thin, brilliant, and of various colors. The most beautiful are known by the following names: Che-pi-lou (green serpent skin), Chen-yu-hoang (yellow of the eel), Ki-tsouf (pale blue or azure), Hoang-tien-pan (spotted yellow); and the vases recorded as made at the time have the following enamels: pale yellow, pale violet, pale green, red soufflé, and blue soufflé (the powdered blue).

The progress made during the reign of the Emperor Khang-he was most important. It is particularly interesting to us, since we are now able to solve certain doubtful points in the Chinese records; for we possess the products themselves, in all their integrity and whiteness of paste, besides their enamels, which are infallible tests.

Decorated porcelains easily betray their origin to the eye of the connoisseur by their tones of color, and the rendering of the design. Moreover, most of the white paste of the period of Khang-he is purer and clearer than that of other periods.

This period is especially remarkable for the lustrous green glaze produced by oxide of copper, of which the transparency and brightness are inimitable. Under no other reign have ceramists succeeded in producing this translucent, iridescent green enamel. The greens of other periods are more superficial, and duller, while the color of this epoch exhibits an incomparable vigor in over-glaze painting.

Among the enamels, the following colors figure with much distinction under this period: the peach-skin, or so-called "peach-blow," "crushed strawberry," "sang de bœuf," "sang de poulet," liver reds (derived from oxide of copper), white, yellow, orange, powder-blue, coral red, salamander red (both the last derived from oxide of iron), céladon, mirror black, apple-green, pea-green, pistache-green, cobalt blue, café au lait, lavender, camellia green, olive, violet, gray, and turquoise blue.

In the period of Yung-tching (A.D. 1723–1735) the director, Nien-hi-yao, abbreviated " Nien,"had charge of the Imperial factory of King-te-tchin. He personally chose all the material. The painters, attracted by the magnificent tone-effect of the chloride-of-gold carmine, attended to all the rose-colors, not only flowers, but animals, horses, furniture, and the like. This important innovation introduced a new variety, with felicitous effects. This uniform tone easily superseded the greens of the preceding periods. The successive predominance of these two colors induced Jacque-mart to group them severally in two classes, the "famille verte" and the " famille rose."

The kaolin products of the kilns of this time, especially those of King-te-tchin, are models in respect of purity of material, graceful forms and beautiful decoration.

The fourth Emperor, Khien-long, or Chien-lung (A.D. 1736–1795), the successor of Yung-tchin, loved porcelain, and protected the ceramic industry with royal munificence during the sixty years of his reign, when he abdicated. During that period a great quantity of fine porcelain was made, much of which exhibits varied and carefully drawn decoration.

Chinese records state that in this period there flourished a porcelain maker named Thang-ing, who seemed to surpass all others, especially in his imitation of antique vases, and

in the ingenious character of his inventions. In the sixth
year of the period Yung-tching, A.D. 1728–1735, Than-ing
established himself at King-te-tchin, as joint decorator with
Nien-hi-yao above-mentioned, where he acquired a brilliant
reputation.

These two distinguished men for a long time conducted
the imperial works; but Thang had better knowledge of the
materials, and greater skill in the firing. Each piece produced was remarkable for manipulation, form and colors.
He succeeded wonderfully well in reproducing the most
precious enamels, and invented a number of new colors
used in the glazing. The Emperor, by special decree,
directed him to illustrate the manufacture of porcelain, and
his illustrations have been copied in the work of M. Stanislas
Julien.

As there is no object in the Garland collection later than
the period of Khien-long, we close our sketch at this point.
Later manufacturers appear to have diminished in excellence; and the destruction caused by the rebellion of
the Tai-Pings not only greatly interfered with the production, but brought about the ruin of the most celebrated of
the factories, that of King-te-tchin. As already stated, the
native accounts do not furnish much information that can
be rendered available; but they show very clearly that the
porcelain-makers have at all times been in the habit of
copying the works of their predecessors, in some instances
so as to impose upon the best judges of their own country.

ETYMOLOGY OF THE WORD PORCELAIN.

It is a singular fact that China, although the creator of so
marvelous a product, so pleasant to the eye, so worthy as an
adjunct to our most luxurious surroundings, should not likewise have given it its name. It remained for western countries to call it porcelain.

The word "pourcelain" is often found in mediæval French
inventories, applied to many different objects, and evidently

was used to specify all kinds of carved vases or utensils made of shells or mother-of-pearl.

The word has undergone sundry unimportant transformations at the hands of the writers of past ages, who gave the name to Oriental porcelain, probably because it resembled shell. At least, this seems to be the accepted hypothesis. The word porcelain is possibly of Italian origin, and derived from the similarity of the glazed white surface to that of the cowrie shell (porcellana).

Jacquemart and Fiquier believed the word porcelain to be derived from the Portuguese porçolana, or porcolla, vessel.

In China porcelain is termed Yao, a word signifying an object baked in a kiln, whether glazed porcelain or glazed pottery. This word came into use from the Thang dynasty (A.D. 618), when the paste became more translucent and white, through the use of kaolin. The word Thao was used before that epoch, and probably refers to a primitive kind of pottery or stone ware. The Chinese also called a kind of porcelain "Tse," whence some writers erroneously interpret the word Tse-khi as porcelain, ignoring or ignorant of the fact that this word designates a porcelain made from a stone called Tse-chi, found in the district Tse-tcheou.

In A.D. 1171 we first find a clear mention of porcelain outside of China. In that year Saladin sent to Nureddin a present of forty pieces of Chinese porcelain. The port of Canton was visited by the Arabs about the ninth century; and they possibly were the first to bring porcelains from China. At that epoch porcelain is said to have been more or less gray, that is, not made wholly of kaolin. A century later, we learn of pieces appearing in Europe, that were more nearly white.

Marco Polo, in 1280, visited one of the sites of porcelain manufacture, and states that it was exported to all parts of the world. It was probably he through whom the attention of his countrymen was called to this product of the far East. Other travelers, of the fourteenth and fifteenth centuries, likewise noted it. It probably reached Europe through

Egypt; at any rate, a present of porcelain vases was sent by the Sultan of Egypt, in 1487, to Lorenzo de' Medici. The Portuguese, however, doubtless made the first direct importation of Chinese wares into Europe, after which the various India Companies of Holland, England, France and Sweden soon followed.

COMPOSITION AND MANUFACTURE OF PORCELAIN.

Porcelain is distinguished from other ceramic products by its whiteness, transparency and vitrification. It is generally divided into two classes: hard and soft paste.

Porcelain proper has a pure white body, is translucent and sonorous, impermeable to water, and not scratched by steel. It is formed of two materials, writes Père d'Entrecolles; one called pè-tun, a fine white fusible substance (a mixture of feldspar and quartz), formerly obtained from the mountain Ma-tsang, in Lin-tching, department of Feouliang. That supply was exhausted in the time of Wan-li (A.D. 1573–1619), but the material was afterwards found at three other places in the same district.

" The stone petrosilex (pè-tun) is crushed in large mortars and pounded to fine powder, then put into a large jar or vat filled with water, stirred, and allowed to rest for a short time, after which the scum which rises is skimmed off and put into another vessel. The dregs of the first jar are taken out and pounded over again; the process being repeated until all the finer parts are removed. After settling, the water in the last jar is carefully drawn off, and the remaining sediment or paste is pressed into large forms and dried. Before it is quite hard it is divided up into small cakes or bricks. These are the pè-tun-tse, or " White Clay Bricks."

The other material is kaolin, so called from its locality; its name being derived from the mountain Kao-ling, near King-te-tchin. Kaolin is a hydrated silicate of alumina, and, by itself, infusible. It is derived from decomposed feldspar. This material requires less work in its preparation. It is found in mines in the mountains, covered with red earth. It is purified by successive washings; generally soaked in water and strained, first through a fine sieve, then through a fine silken bag, made double. It is then placed in a case or box formed of newly baked bricks, and covered with cloth. After draining, the paste thus formed is kneaded and worked until the material is thoroughly compact, and then made into small bricks like the pè-tun-tse. These bricks are marked or stamped by the makers, and sold in this shape to the ceramist. Sometimes counterfeit marks are put upon an inferior article. For this reason, writes Père d'Entrecolles, the stamps of certain families of reputation are especially in request.

These pè-tun-tse bricks are broken up by the potter, and thrown into a large vessel of water to dissolve. The kao-lin, dry and in bricks, is put without breaking into a wicker basket, within a jar of water, where it easily dissolves.

The feldspar gives the transparency, but by itself alone would fall apart in the kiln. The kao-lin is the material that gives plasticity and strength. The mixture of kao-lin and pè-tun-tse in equal portions is used for porcelain of the finest quality; four parts kao-lin to six of pè-tun-tse, for the second quality; one part kao-lin to three of pè-tun-tse, for the third.

The mixture is made into paste with water, compressed, rolled and kneaded on a table, and beaten to remove air bubbles. It is then ready for the potter's wheel or table, where it receives its principal form, by turning, in its soft state.

The portions that cannot be turned on a wheel, such as handles, and other attachments, are separately moulded and fastened on with layers of paste and a bit of gum. After the surface is smoothed, relief ornamentation, if any, is added; and the piece is put away to dry. Large objects are generally made in two or three parts, joined together by moistened paste. While the foot is still unwrought, there is added the decoration in blue or other colors which require to be highly fired. The glaze is next applied, either by dipping or blowing with a tube. This strengthens the object sufficiently to permit the workman to fashion the foot on a wheel, and to inscribe a mark. As soon as these last are coated with glaze, the piece is ready for the kiln.

The pieces, packed in clay seggars to protect them from injury, are placed in the furnace in such a way that each piece may receive its proper degree of heat; the smaller pieces filling all the available spaces.

The kiln (called *Chao-yao*) is bricked up; the fires lighted, and carefully continued till the baking, which must be gradual and slow, is completed. The temperature varies according to the fusibility and the glaze; the time required is from 35 to 36 hours. It is necessary both to reach and to stop at the proper point; and for testing they draw out some small pieces through small openings. When the necessary point is reached, they close all the little openings, and stop the fire. It requires four to five days for the oven to cool so as to be opened for the removal of the pieces. In this state the porcelain is beautiful, in its transparent white glaze.

There are two modes of applying colored decoration on porcelain; "over the glaze," and "under the glaze," painting. In each method the "high" or "low" or "muffled" firing is used, according to the colors employed. The work of painting is divided up among a large number of workmen, each one confined to his special details. One traces the flowers, another paints them, a third paints mountains or animals, a fourth paints figures, and so on. Gilding is done by still another, at the same stage with the painting. The object is then baked again. The glaze is made of pè-tun mixed with fern ashes and lime. Other materials are often used; for instance *hoa-chi* (steatite), sometimes with the glaze, and sometimes in the paste. Yeou-ko is another substance used in the same way.

EXTRACTS FROM PERE D'ENTRECOLLES.

Père d'Entrecolles, Missionary of the Society of Jesus, arrived in China in 1700, whence he wrote letters from Jao-tcheou, in the province of Feou-liang, about the town of King-te-tchin, where the imperial factory of porcelain was situated. In a letter dated September 1st, 1712, he wrote that while his curiosity would not have led him to study the subject of the production of porcelain, he felt that it might be of service to Europe, and therefore availed himself of his opportunities. " The town of King-te-tchin," he writes, "is only three miles distant from, and a dependency of, Feou-liang, which is a dependency of Jao-tcheou, and is situated in a plain, surrounded by high mountains; the one to the east, against which the town is built, is outwardly in form of a semi-circle; and from the two adjacent mount-ains issue two rivers which unite. One is small, the other very large, and their confluence forms a magnificent port over three miles in length; a vast basin wherein the river loses much of its velocity. Frequently in this large harbor are moored two or three rows of junks. Entering the port, the sight is greeted by immense volumes of smoke and flames, which mark the outlines of the town, against the crescent of mountains in the background, whose relative position may perhaps be the reason that King-te-tchin has surpassed all other localities in the production of porcelain.

"Junks also arrive at King-te-tchin, laden with a white substance called 'yeou-ko' (oil), although 'tsi' (glaze) would better apply; which is made from a very hard stone. It can be produced from the same stone as the pè-tun, selecting pieces having green spots. The history of Feou-liang says the best stone for the 'oil' (glaze) has spots of the color of cypress leaves, or is of a brown color, with reddish spots like toad-flax. To this, reduced to powder, is added one per cent of a mineral resembling alum, called chi-kao. Yeou-ko is always mixed with ten per cent of an 'oil' (glaze) made from the cinders of quicklime and ferns burned together. Formerly persimmon wood was also burned with the lime, but this has become so scarce that it is no longer used; which is, perhaps, one of the causes of the superiority of the ancient porcelain. Merchants who sell the yeou-ko frequently cheat by making it from other substances; and some manufacturers use even thirty per cent of 'oil' made from cinders; but their products are very inferior.

"In the matter of colors for porcelain, they have a great number. In Europe we generally see only a bright blue on white ground, whereas the Chinese have a great variety. * * * * They make some of solid red and of different shades and appearances, those of 'oily' red soufflé having the appearance of being stippled. When these pieces are successful, which is very seldom, they are highly prized, and command a large price. There are also objects on which landscapes are painted in many colors and relieved with gilding; these are made very beautiful if you are willing to pay a large price, but ordinary pieces of this kind are not to be compared with their blue and white. The annals of King-te-tchin say that in ancient times the people only used white porcelain; this was probably because at that time the stone was not yet found, near Jao-tcheou, from which the blue is made. That now used for fine pieces comes from a great distance and is very costly. It is reported that a Chinese merchant was once wrecked on a desert coast, where he found more riches than he lost, his find being an azure stone; he built a vessel, loaded it with these stones and brought them home; and never was such a color seen before or since at King-te-tchin. He, however, was never able to find his desert coast again.

"While the body porcelain is naturally white, and the 'oil' (glaze) with which they cover it increases this whiteness, still, on certain pieces, they apply a surface-white in combination with other color decorations. This white is made from a transparent stone, by calcination in the furnace; and azure blue is produced by the same process. Red is made from copperas. Green is made by adding to an ounce of white lead and a half ounce of stone powder, three ounces of what I think to be the purest scales from hammered copper. Green thus prepared becomes the matrix of violet, which is produced by adding white. Yellow is made of seven parts of white and three of copperas. These colors do not appear upon their application, but only after the second baking.

"The red is applied by mixing it with the ordinary glaze and a glaze made of a white stone. Perfect pieces of this color are very highly esteemed; when struck they do not ring. The soufflé is made by using a little tube, one end of which is covered with a very fine gauze. This end is gently dipped into the prepared color; the artist brings it near the object, and blows through the other end; this is repeated until the desired effect is produced.

"Such objects are very rare and highly esteemed. Black porcelain is also esteemed, and resembles our burning mirrors. Decoration in gold upon the black enriches the color. Objects are also made surrounded by a shell of open-work, forming one solid piece with the inner one. I have also seen porcelain decorated with Chinese and Tartar female figures in the most exquisite manner, resembling enamels.

"If no other glaze is used than that made from white stones, crackle ware is produced. The glaze gives a grayish white color by itself, but it will produce the same effect on pieces which have been colored. Gold is applied with a brush after mixing it with white lead in gummy water. * * *

"Objects of porcelain are also made which are very delicate and thin, but are nevertheless moulded into most difficult shapes. In order to effect this, the interior is shaped on the wheel, glazed and baked. The object is again placed on the wheel, and the exterior worn away by grinding until the desired thinness is obtained, when the exterior is also glazed, and the piece is painted, glazed and baked again. Before applying the glaze, the surface is smoothed to a polish with a very fine brush, which is passed over it again and again. Great skill is required in glazing very thin porcelain. The interior is first sprinkled with the glaze and allowed to dry, after which the outside is dipped into it. The bottom is left solid during this operation; it is then hollowed out on the wheel.

"Objects for export to Europe are mostly made upon new models, often whimsical and difficult to execute. * * * * Some of those made for the Chinese are also very remarkable; the Heir Apparent ordered a large lantern made of one piece of openwork, so that when a lamp was placed inside, it illuminated the whole room.

"The Chinese are great antiquarians; indeed in this respect they surpass all other nations. The date-marks upon porcelain can scarcely be relied upon, and much of the finest antique porcelain bears no mark at all. Hence the antiquarian has to rely upon his taste, to select his gems by form and color. Of course tradition bears its value; thus the smallest object of pottery used by the Emperors Yao or Chun, who reigned several centuries before the Tangs, under whom the first porcelain was made for the Emperors, commands in China an enormous price.

"The annals of King-te-tchin inform us that in ancient times, as at present, objects of various prices were produced; thus certain urns are mentioned each of which was sold for 59 taels, that is 80 écus. [An écu, or crown, equals $1.20, and in 1712 had about five times its money value of to-day. This would make each of these objects cost about $500.]

"Quite recently a new material has been found which can be substituted for kaolin; it is called hoa-chi, and is a kind of stone, or rather chalk, of about the consistence of hard soap. Porcelain made of this material is very expensive. [A kind of soft paste is referred to.] It is very brittle, and difficult to bake, but offers the most desirable surface for the artist to paint, and retains the colors perfectly. For this reason the body of the piece is frequently made of common material, and a surface of this hoa-chi is obtained by dipping the piece into a liquid preparation of it. It is also much lighter than the average porcelain. Where the kaolin costs but 20 sous, the hoa-chi costs an écu. Another use of this hoa-chi is very beautiful in effect; after it is prepared in little grains it is diluted with water to the consistence of paste, and by means of a brush tracings are made on the surface of objects before they are glazed; after glazing and baking, these tracings appear of a different whiteness from the body of the porcelain. This whiteness of the hoa-chi is called Siang-ya-pe or white of ivory. The chikao (a mineral resembling alum) is used in the same way for white tracings, but it cannot, like the hoa-chi, be substituted for kaolin in the body of the porcelain.

"Medallions are left to be otherwise decorated by applying pieces of wet paper to the object, dipping the object in the tsi-kin, and when nearly dry, removing the paper; this leaves white medallions, which are decorated to suit the fancy; then the object is glazed and baked. * * *

"A kind of glaze called tsouï-yeou produces innumerable little cracks over the surface when applied alone. It renders the object very brittle, and destroys its ringing tone when struck, but when mixed with other glazes it does not. * * * The mixture used to produce the peculiar black carries its own glaze and requires the most careful baking; pieces of this color must be placed in the very centre of the furnace, where the heat is most uniform.

"In the present year (1722), on account of orders from Europe, vases have been made more than three feet in height. This had been considered impossible; they were made, however, in three pieces which were so nicely united that you could not discover the joints. Of 80 vases of this description placed in the kiln, only 8 succeeded, the others proving a total loss."

CATALOGUE OF PORCELAINS.

I. WITH DECORATION OVER THE GLAZE.

This section includes specimens painted with fusible colors, after the glazing has been applied to the white paste and subjected to the proper firing.

Under this head are here classed those pieces of which the decoration is made upon a colored foundation of transparent glaze over the "biscuit," or white paste; though such objects properly form a class by themselves, and have been so recognized in China for centuries. The kind here under consideration has always held a high place in private collections and museums, and still ranks among the most highly prized productions of the ceramic art of the Far East.

The order of description here followed is that of the numbering of the cases.

CASE 1.

Examples of the characteristic type produced in China under the Mings; its painting chiefly in flat and unshaded colors. During the later periods of that dynasty, and especially under the Emperor Khang-he (A.D. 1661–1723), the specimens show more refinement and delicacy in the handling of translucent colors.

This case contains fifty-eight objects; the predominant decoration in green enamel. Several of the specimens well exemplify the high technical skill attained during the XV., XVI. and XVII. centuries. The following are especially noteworthy:

Very Tall Vase, directly in the centre of the case; cylindrical; decoration, a hunting scene outside the walls of an imperial city. Mounted warriors in pursuit of wild animals; with mountainous landscape; in polychrome on white ground. Khang-he period, A.D. 1661-1722.

Two Large Jars, with covers, on the central shelf. Figure-subjects, vigorously rendered in polychrome, on a white paste of fine texture. Khang-he period.

Two Tall Vases, of graceful-beaker form, to the right and left, respectively, of the two preceding. The one has white medallions embellished with flowers, fruit, birds and *ky-lins;* within a ground of stippled green, on which are flowers and butterflies. The other vase has similar decoration, with the addition of various animals and symbolic devices. Same period as the last.

Four Tall Vases, of form similar to the last; one in each lower corner; all differently decorated. Two have historical figure-subjects, illustrating court-tribute and presentations; the third, warriors; the fourth, medallions, with branches of trees, flowers and birds, in polychrome on a white ground. Khang-he period, A.D. 1661-1722.

Two Vases, cylindrical; on the lower tier at the end. The one has a series of white medallions with landscapes and figures; about which are butterflies and flowers in various colors, on a foundation of lustrous green glaze. The other has diagonal arabesque borders, forming panels that enclose landscapes in polychrome on a white ground. Khang-he period.

Two Vases, of like cylindrical form, on the lower tier at the end opposite the last, have their entire surfaces covered with landscape and figure-subjects, in polychrome. Khang-he period. (From the Leyland collection, London.)

Cylindrical Vase, of same type with the last. Medallions, with warriors and horsemen in polychrome, within a red ground of flowers and arabesques. On the same tier, an

Oviform Vase, decorated with warriors, in polychrome. Khang-he period.

Gourd-shaped Vase; superb white paste, covered with thin transparent glaze. Medallions, leaf and fruit-shaped, embellished with various flowers. The upper portion has white scroll-shaped panels with landscapes, flowers, etc. The paste and decoration exemplify the highest type of this class. Khang-he period, A. D. 1661–1722.

Two Square Vases, with quadrangular panels; small sprigs with fruit forming the handles; profusely decorated with conventional peonies and leaf-arabesques, in which the red, blue, yellow, purple and green appear in unusual excellence. Stands of teakwood. Khang-he period.

Among the objects in this case which have a colored-glaze foundation over the " biscuit," or paste, are :

Two Vases, flat baluster-shape ; with small handles formed of slender dragons. Decoration, a floral subject in polychrome, on a light amber-colored ground. Tching-hwa (Ming) period, A. D. 1465–1488.

Two Vases, of like flat baluster-form, without handles; white leaf-shaped medallions decorated with flowers, birds and various objects, within a yellow and green diaper ground. Ming dynasty.

Two Water Vases, cylindrical, with brass spouts, and affixed masks for handles; decorated with horses in purple, yellow and green; encircled with yellow bands. Ming dynasty.

Water Vase, like the last, but without spout; similar decoration with horses; white bands. Ming dynasty.

Small Vase ; unique ; baluster-shaped; water-lily decoration in various glazes on a ground of amber yellow. Ming dynasty.

Pair of Large Figures of the Dog "Fo," in polychrome glaze, with decoration of striking brilliancy; raised on high bases; embellished with butterflies, etc. Ming dynasty.

Another Pair, smaller; mounted in gilt bronze.

A Third Pair, with like coloring and decoration.

Two Parrots, decorated in various colors. Ming dynasty.

Vase; unique; baluster-shape; small dragon handles in

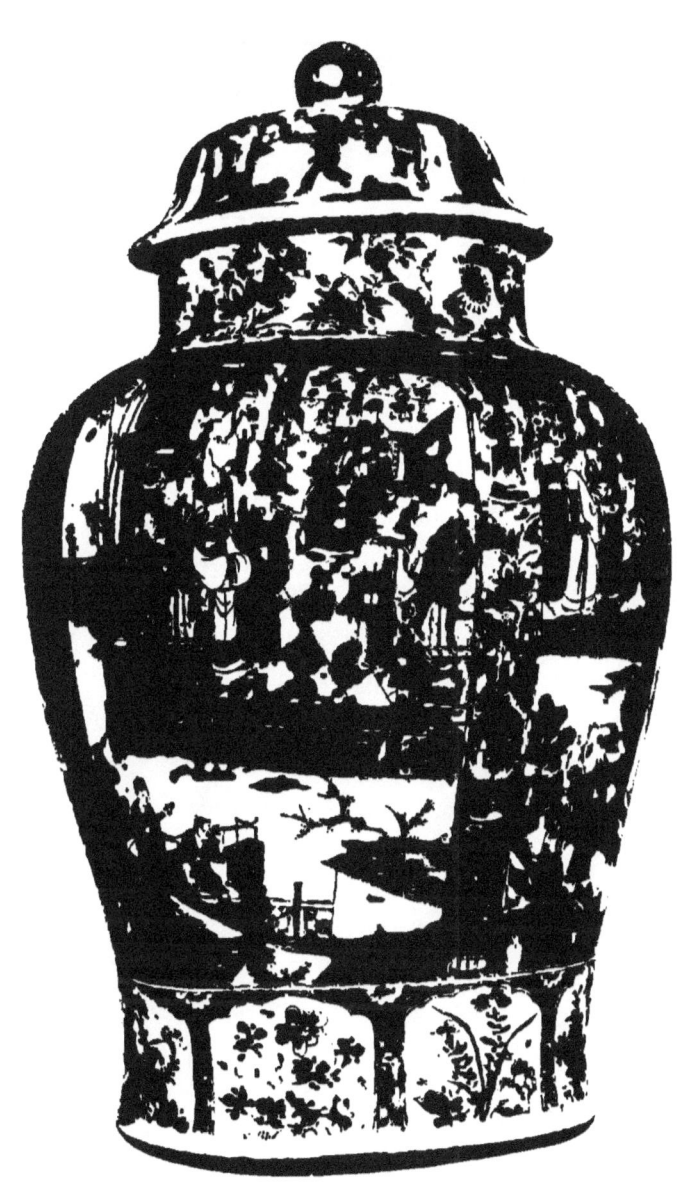

CASE 1.

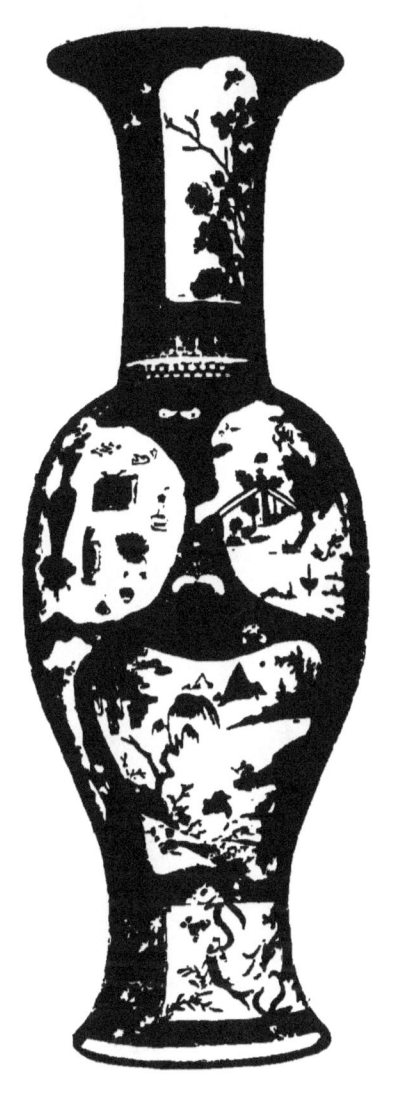

CASE 1.

CASSEL.

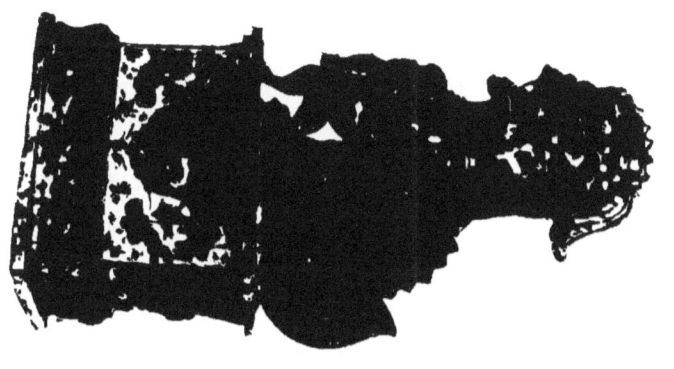

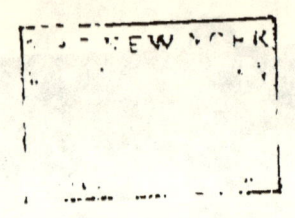

free relief; glazed with a lustrous, transparent green enamel, resembling in color the *Fai-tsouf* (a precious light green jade). Date-mark, Kea-tsing (A.D. 1522–1567), written in a horizontal line under the upper edge.

The Large Bowl, on the lower shelf, displays a figure-subject of court ladies engaged in their pastimes, rendered in delicately colored glazes on a white surface of fine texture. Khang-he period.

Vase, square; medallions in free relief over a decorated arabesque ground ; metal mounting (small rim) at top. Khang-he period, A.D. 1661–1722.

Pair of Candlesticks, formed of crouching figures holding cups over their heads; decorated in various colors, chiefly red. Made for India, during the Khang-he period.

Pair of Small Seated Figures; polychrome decoration.

Small Tablet, decorated. Teakwood stand.

The remainder of the contents of this case are small vases and bowls, decorated in polychrome.

CASE 2.

Objects enameled on a colored foundation. Included are XV., XVI. and XVII. century porcelains with a black ground, in which the design is always in " reserve," i. e. in portions from which the black ground is excluded; embellished by designs in transparent enamels, among which the blossom of the *Mei-hwa* tree (a prunus) often predominates—whence they are often (incorrectly) called " black hawthorn." This decoration has for centuries been applied upon both biscuit and pure white kaolin paste. The color of the black enamel is developed and fixed under the action of a high or central fire, of intensity suited to the degrees of fusibility of the metallic oxides used to produce the colors. For the dull colors is employed white lead mixed with oxides of manganese, cobalt and copper. The brilliant black is obtained from the oxides of manganese and cobalt, with a mixture of uranite and ochre. The fixing of the black glaze upon the paste taxed the utmost skill of the ancient ceramists; and their productions remain to-day unrivaled. The number of metallic oxides used for the other colors—in varying mixture —is limited; but the Chinese ceramists knew how to combine them so as to obtain almost the tints of oil painting.

Case 2 comprises sixty-three examples. Some tall vases, jars and beakers, with certain small objects, bear the Tching-hwa mark (A.D. 1465–1487); others show the characteristic paste of Wan-li (A.D. 1573–1619); others possess all the characteristics of the Khang-he period (A.D. 1661–1722).

Among the larger pieces are to be especially noted:

Large Jar, with cover, profusely decorated with birds, plants and flowers; the magnolia, hydrangea and peony predominating, in brilliant colors on a ground of lustrous black enamel. (From the Orrock collection, London.) On either side of this jar are:

Tall Vases, of graceful beaker form; one with flowers and birds, similar to the last; the other with prunus blossoms in light-colored reserved spaces, their stems and leaves, with birds, in brilliant colors,—on a lustrous iridescent black ground.

Four Vases, similar to the last, of tall beaker form, one in each corner of the middle tier; each with its distinct decoration of flowers and birds; on a black ground of varying depth.

Another Vase, of similar form, in the middle tier below the large jar. This has the small blossoms picked out in mazarine blue glaze; the branches and foliage in natural colors, beside green-covered rocks, with birds, on a deep black ground.

Another Vase, of like form, in a place corresponding to the last, on the front or gallery side. Peach blossoms painted in strong pinkish-red enamel; on a deep lustrous black ground. This piece is unique, and is known as the

CASE 2.

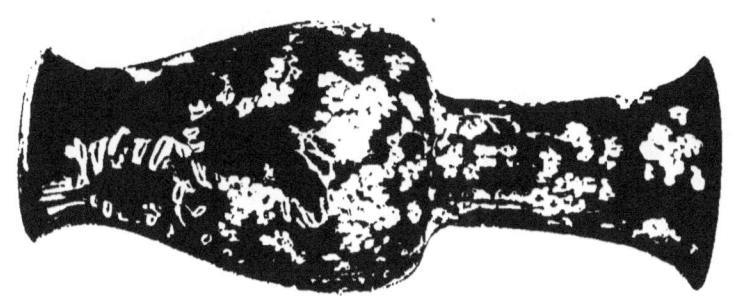

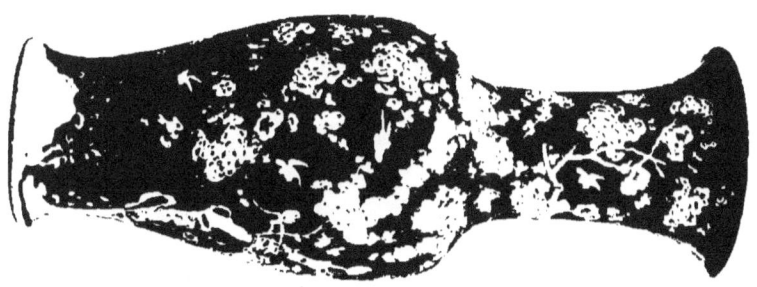

"Red Hawthorn Vase." (Formerly in the South Kensington Museum, London.)

Tall Green Vase, beaker form. Branches, buds and blossoms of the prunus; delicately outlined in reserve, in light-colored glaze on a green ground of transparent texture. Unique. Ming dynasty.

Two Jars, with covers; in the lower corners of the case. White floral medallions, outlined in red, on a black ground. Khang-he period. (From the Leyland collection.)

Two Vases, square baluster-shape; one with, the other without, handles (with the three tall vases on the middle tier). Floral painting, of pronounced character and dignity, relieved by a black ground of waxy texture. Ming dynasty.

Two Square Vases, in which each side has an individual treatment. Lotus, magnolia, peony and prunus blossoms predominate; in natural colors on a deep black ground. Ming dynasty.

Two Vases of quadrangular body, tapering downwards, and cylindrical neck (on the opposite side of same tier). Each panel decorated with a special emblematic flower (chrysanthemum, prunus, lotus and peony, respectively) in natural colors, relieved by a soft black ground. Ming dynasty.

Three Beakers, corresponding in general character to the two jars in the lower corners of the case; decorated medallions, the prunus blossom predominating, on black ground. Khang-he period.

Vase, baluster-form (third corner). Two dragons, in various colors, on a deep black ground.

Teapot, on lower shelf; in the form of the symbolical character "*chou*" (longevity). Face in light green, with blossoms: the two sides enameled in black ground, with decoration. Unique. Ming dynasty.

Square Vase; two sides decorated with landscapes in polychrome; the alternate ones in green, with inscriptions, framed in black bands. Ming dynasty. (From a Paris collection.)

Bowl; green glaze with magnolia decoration. Ming dynasty. (From the Orrock collection.)

Bowl; olive glaze with blossom decoration.

Small Bottle; green arabesque design on a black ground. Khang-he period, A.D. 1661-1722.

Small Vase; green arabesque design on black ground.

Small Vase, baluster-shape; soft black ground, and prunus decoration in reserve. Khang-he period, A.D. 1661-1722.

Buddhistic Figure, Si-wang-mou, the queen of the genii of longevity, holding the sacred *Ling-tchi* in her hand, and seated on the lotus thalamus, with porcelain base. Ming dynasty.

Porcelain Tablet, in form of a screen, decorated with blossoms on a black ground. Teak wood stand.

The small vases, cups, and animal figures are of the Ming dynasty.

CASE 3.

The specimens in this case exhibit a great variety of color-painting over the glaze; but chiefly noteworthy are the pieces with rose enamel, which derives its tint from chloride of gold, and was first invented under the Thsing dynasty. (Some writers claim it for the end of the Khang-he period, A.D. 1661-1722; others for the next later period, Yung-tching, A.D. 1723-1735. We learn from the history of King-te-tchin that many new colors were invented during both reigns, which are often referred to as the time of the renaissance of art in China.) In most of the specimens in this case the rose color is predominant, but some are of the green variety, belonging to the latter part of the Ming dynasty and the Khang-he period.

Among the sixty-two pieces are to be specially noted:

Large Jar, with cover, in the centre of the upper tier. Decoration, enameled black ground, green arabesque foliage, and conventional rose-colored chrysanthemums; leaf-shaped medallions in white reserve, embellished with flowers, birds

CASE 2.

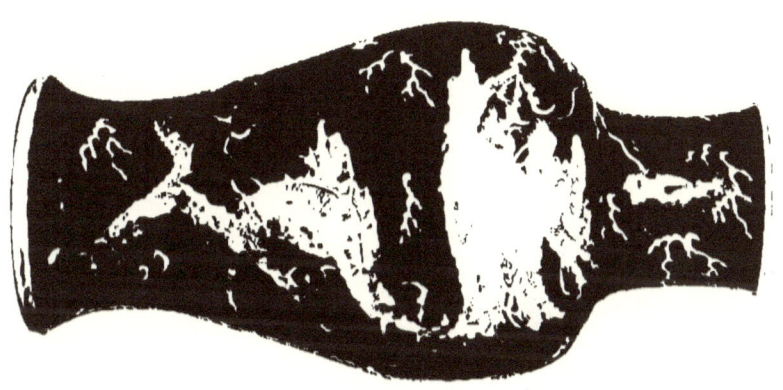

CASE 3.

and animals, in delicate natural colors. Neck and base encircled by fretted borders. Yung-tching period. (From the Marlborough collection. A companion piece is shown in Case 22.)

Four Jars, with covers, in the corners of the upper tier. Brilliant greenish-black ground, with arabesque foliage in transparent green, and conventional chrysanthemums in delicate rose enamels. The larger reserve medallions are of various forms, with landscapes, flowers and birds. Different borders, about the foot and neck of each; and each surmounted by the dog Fo. (Two of these jars are from the Marlborough collection.)

Three Jars, with covers, on the lower tier; smaller than the last; with similar greenish-black ground and decorations; but differing in the borders at neck and base, and in the various polychrome medallions.

Two Beakers, of the same style of decoration.

Five small pieces—three covered jars and two vases; decorated in light-colored enamels on a rose-colored ground. (From the Marquis collection, Paris.)

Two Jars, with covers. Delicate rose-tinted enamel ground, with fine white floral medallions. Neck-mounting of gilt bronze. (Marquis collection.)

Beaker, of like color with the last, with arabesque decorations of unusual excellence.

Two Plates; similar decorations, with polychrome.

Two Figurines; one, the demon Kouei-sing, on the head of a dragon; the other, a young lady in court attire, in polychrome, the rose tint predominant.

Among the smaller pieces are several egg-shell plates, cups and saucers, all of the Yung-tching period.

The following are of the Khang-he period:

Two Spherical Bottles, with long necks, in the two lower corners; one with figures of divinities, on a fine white ground; the other, representations of the dog Fo, in various colors on a white ground. (From the Leyland collection, London.)

Two Tall Vases, baluster-form, in the corners opposite the last. The Chinese character *"show"* in tessellated or fret detail on a white ground; the reserve medallions, enclosing Taoist divinities, painted in various transparent colors.

Cylindrical Vase; butterflies in various colors, on a white ground.

Large Plaque; butterflies in various colors, on a stippled green ground, with similar border.

Two Bowls, decorated in colors on a *café au lait* (color of coffee with milk) ground.

Tall Square Vase; black medallions; worn gold decoration; landscape in translucent colors.

Tall Cylindrical Vase, on front centre shelf. Landscape decoration in polychrome, on amber-yellow ground.

Plaque; dragons of archaic design, on a tessellated ground; green color predominant; on biscuit. Ming dynasty.

CASE 4.

Specimens with polychrome decoration, in which predominates the rose-colored enamel of the Yung-tching period (A.D. 1723-1735). A few specimens, with the predominant translucent green, are of the Khang-he period, A.D. 1661-1772. The case contains ninety-three pieces. The largest piece is a

Great Jar, with cover. Deep-rose-colored scalloped borders at base and neck, over a white body embellished with floral offerings vigorously depicted in green, pink, and other light colors. Yung-tching period, A.D. 1723-1735. (From a Portuguese collection.)

Other noteworthy pieces are:

Two Jars, with covers, on either side of the preceding. Deep-rose color, with reserve medallions and scrolls, showing a paste of fine texture. In the circular panel, a Chinese sage, with a boy, and sundry accessories. In the fan-shaped medallions, flowers in bloom, and brilliant-feathered poultry;

CASE 3.

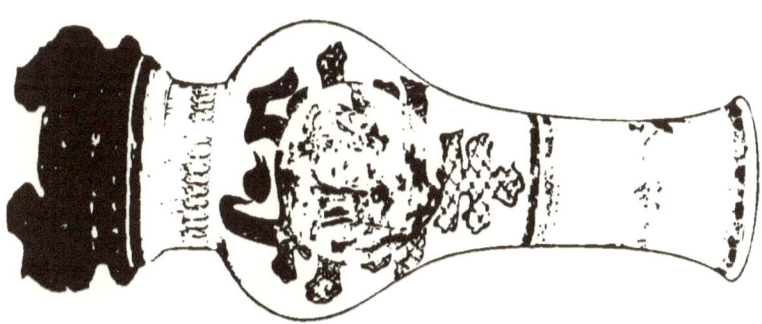

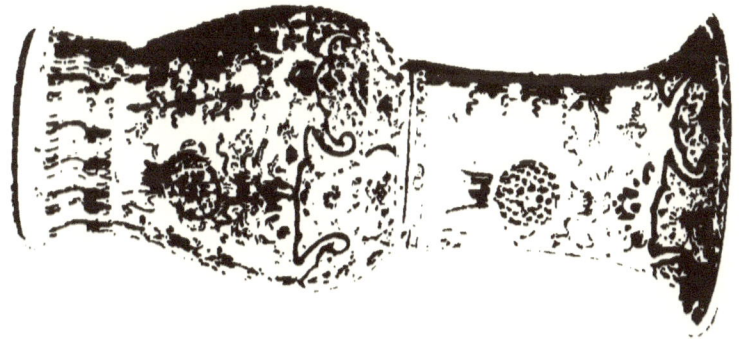

in the white scrolls, flowers and birds, in delicate colors; over the rose-colored field, conventional chrysanthemums and their sprays, in various hues. Narrow geometrical borders about neck, base and cover. Yung-tching period. (From a Portuguese collection.)

Two Jars, similar to the last, but smaller, in the corner of the middle tier.

Two Jars, similar to the last, in the lower corners. (From the Wells collection.)

Two Vases, ovoid form, in the lower corners. Ground, light pink *soufflé* (i.e. formed by blowing the color through a tube); with floral and arabesque decoration in various colors. Yung-tching period.

Large Bowl, in centre of lower shelf. Deep-rose-colored exterior, with scalloped and fretted band in green. Interior, floral gift-offerings in natural tints on a white ground. Yung-tching period, A.D. 1723-1735. (From Lord Revelstoke's collection.)

Five Small Pieces, on lower shelf. Floral medallions; rose-color predominant. Yung-tching period.

Two Figures, each holding a lotus flower. Rose-colored robes, with decoration in polychrome enamels.

Hawk, and Cock. Rose-colored enamel predominant in the decoration. Yung-tching period, A.D. 1723-1735.

Tall Oviform Vase, at one end of the case. Rose-colored, *soufflé* enamel, of even texture. Yung-tching period.

Tall Jar, with cover; light green enamel, with white and rose-colored blossoms scattered over the field; leaf-shaped medallions in white reserve, with floral design. Yung-tching period. (From a Holland collection.)

Two Tall Vases, beaker form, gilt-bronze mounting. Sky-blue enameled ground; leaf shaped white medallions with floral embellishments. Yung-tching period.

Hexagonal Vase ; open-work medallions and figures in light polychrome.

Three Small Beakers. Light rose-colored ground; floral medallions.

Two Jars. Floral decoration in polychrome enamels on black ground.

Egg-Shell Plates ; painted in delicate colors; rose-tinted enamel predominant.

Egg-Shell Cups and Saucers, with decorations like the last. Yung-tching period.

Vase, trumpet beaker-shaped; leaf-shaped medallions, on a ground formed by diapered longitudinal polychrome borders. Yung-tching period.

Vase, trumpet beaker-shaped; polychrome medallions of landscapes and flowers, on rose-colored ground. Yung-tching period.

Among the Khang-he specimens with predominating green color are to be mentioned:

Two Tall Bottles ; spherical bodies and long necks; painted with *ky-lins*, on a white body of fine texture. (From the Leyland collection.)

Two Tall Vases, with small handles, in the lower corners. Decoration, landscapes, court figures, etc., on a white ground, showing a brilliant cobalt blue.

On the lower shelf, at the end:

Five Small Pieces, painted in polychrome, with medallions, etc.

Pilgrim Bottle. Phœnix, red, on white ground.

Pilgrim Bottle. Polychrome decoration.

Pair of Bottles. *Café-au-lait* glaze; white floral medallions.

Pair of Vases ; medallions, with figures in polychrome, surrounded by a blue ground, with white butterflies in slight relief. Khien-long period, A.D. 1736-1795.

In the lower portion of this case are shown thirteen plates made in China from foreign designs. In the history of King-te-tchin there are numerous notices of porcelain made for European tastes—referred to in the letters of Père d'Entrecolles (1712-1722), when large pieces were ordered by Canton merchants doing business with Europeans. Many such pieces have on them armorial bearings, of persons or

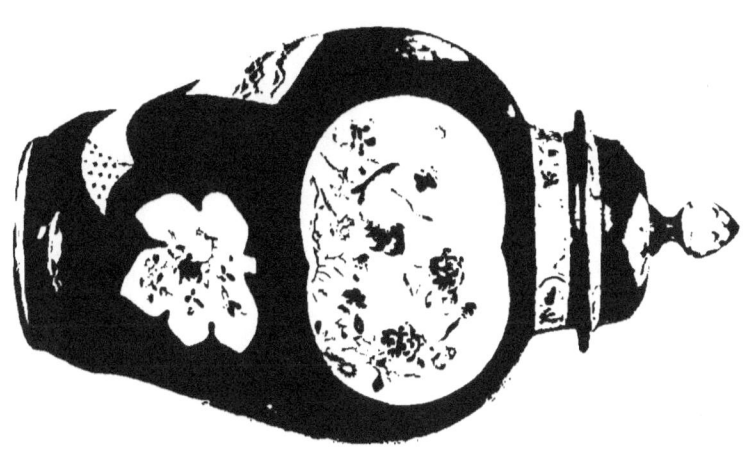

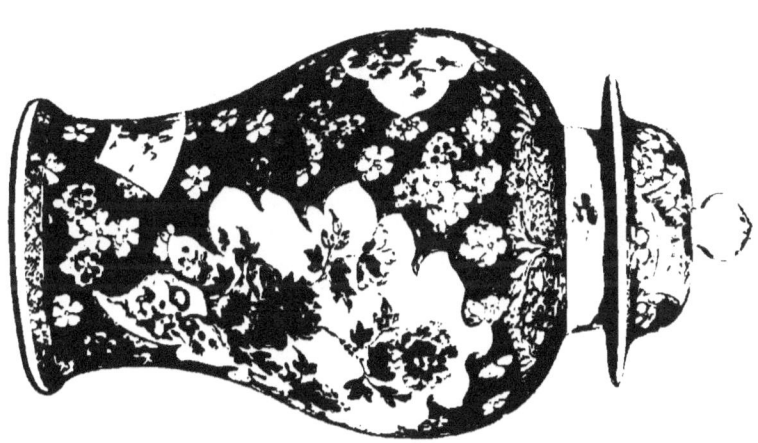

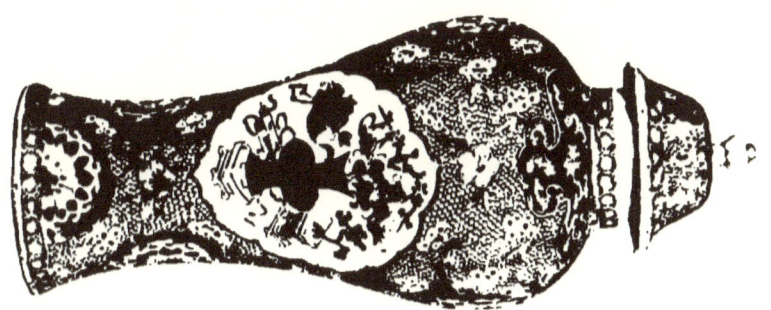

CASE 1.

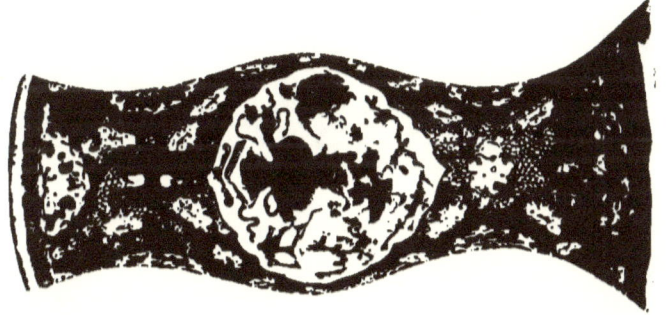

cities, and even of royalty. Those here exhibited bear the arms of cities and guilds, whose names are inscribed on the plates.

CASE 5.

Chiefly specimens with sky-blue *soufflé* ground, and white reserve medallions decorated in cobalt blue in various shades. The colors are all applied under (i.e. before) the glaze, and heightened by the firing—which the oxide of cobalt resists to a very high degree. In productions of this sort the Chinese succeeded in varying the monotone color by various treatment of the surfaces before firing; a clever invention of the time of Khang-he. According to Père d'Entrecolles, the blue used for the *soufflé* surfaces is very carefully prepared from the time it is mined; and only the smaller particles are selected for the first grade. Pieces steeped in this color were never considered as valuable as those with the color deposited by blowing (*soufflé*)—a process requiring the utmost care; and the objects were valued according to the brilliancy of the result. In this process, the color is blown from the extremity of a tube of bamboo, to which is fixed a piece of gauze at one end, on which the prepared color is put by dipping, or with a brush. The tube is then properly directed, and blown from the other end. The fine powdered bits gradually cover the required surface uniformly, or according to the skill of the artist. If reserve spaces are left, these are painted separately.

This Case (5) contains thirty-nine examples of the "powder-blue" variety, with thirty-four pieces painted in blue on white ground; all painted under the glaze.

Of the blue *soufflé* specimens of the Khang-he period (A. D. 1661-1672), the following should be noticed:

Five Pieces, on the upper tier: two jars with covers, and three cylindrical vases. Ground color, lustrous sky-blue *soufflé;* reserve panels, or medallions, painted with landscapes, figures and flowers, in cobalt blue of the purest quality. Khang-he period.

Pair of Tall Bottles, with spherical body and long neck; on lower middle shelf. Ground like the last; reserve medallions with *ky-lins.* Khang-he period.

Cylindrical Vase, in centre of middle tier. Ground, fine *soufflé* blue; landscapes and floral medallions, cobalt blue. Khang-he period.

On the same side, **several small vases and bottles** with similar decoration. Same period.

Two Jars, one with cover, in the lower corners. Deep blue ground; reserve medallions, with vases and various objects, in deep cobalt blue. Same period.

Two Tall Vases, baluster-shaped, in the lower corners. Ground, blue *soufflé;* medallions painted in cobalt blue. Same period.

Water-Bottle, Persian shape. Blue and white medallions on a *soufflé* ground. Same period.

Plate. Blue and white medallions, in a sky-blue ground. Same period.

Tall Bottle, with spherical body. Solid blue *soufflé* glaze. Same period.

Several small bottles and vases are distributed among these larger objects; all of like decoration and period.

Among the blue and white specimens are to be noticed:

Two " Hawthorn " Blossom Ginger Jars, with *chimaera* medallions.

Ginger Jar of like type, with medallions enclosing branches of the prunus in blossom. Khang-he period.

Several plates, of like type in decoration and quality, are seen in this case, together with smaller jars and vases, painted in blue on a white ground.

Tall Vase, baluster form, decorated with a conventional flower of the lily kind, blue on a white ground. Khang-he period.

Two Ovoid Vases, decorated with figures, etc.

Series of Plates ; figure subjects.

Bottle ; lace pattern; tracery in blue.

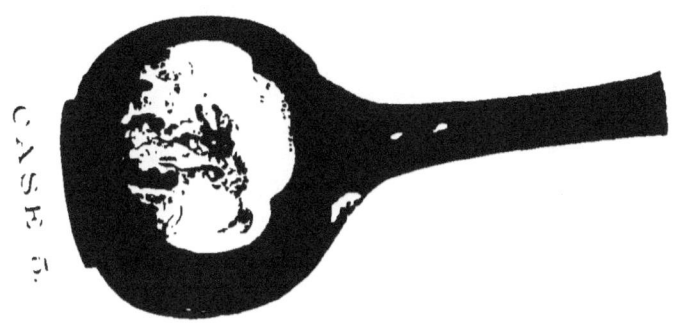

CASE 5.

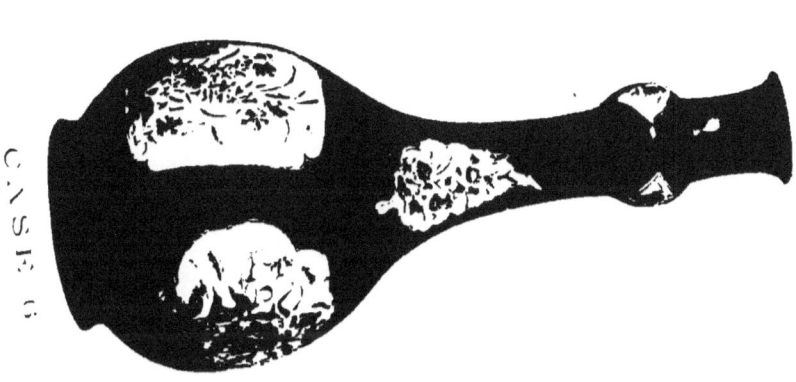

CASE 6.

Two Bottles, with handles; painted in blue under the glaze. XVIII. century.

CASE 6.

Specimens of the blue *soufflé*, or "powder-blue" variety, but differing from those in Case 5 by the painting being over the glaze, in polychrome, on the white medallions. This is done after the first firing. The white reserve spaces are of many forms; as the shape of a leaf, flower, or fruit, the silhouette (shadow-form) of an object, or the *bizarre* form of an animal or person. These forms are made by cutting them out in paper, and fixing them wet on the object, before applying the *soufflé*. The contents of this case are wholly made up of such powder-blue specimens, with over-glaze painting on the panels; the green predominating. There are seventy-six pieces, belonging to the Khang-he period, A.D. 1661–1722. The following are especially noteworthy:

Five Pieces, on the upper shelf; three jars, with covers, and two vases; medallions with landscapes and figures. (From the Wells collection, London.)

Pair of Large Jars, with covers, in two corners of the lower tier. Medallions with landscapes and figure subjects, in polychrome enamels.

Tall Cylindrical Vase, in centre of last-mentioned shelf. Sky-blue ground; red floral medallions.

Tall Spherical-bodied Bottle, on shelf above the last. Fine blue ground; medallions with presentation-objects and flowers, in various colors. (From the Orrock collection.)

Two Tall Cylindrical Vases, on same side with the last; with fine medallions. Near these are **five trumpet-necked bottles**, with fine blue *soufflé* bodies, and floral medallions on the necks.

Two Ovoid Vases, with similar medallions, sundry **smaller bottles**, and **two round boxes** with covers, on the same side of the case, are worthy of notice.

On the opposite side of the case:

Tall Bottle, with spherical body. Lapis-lazuli blue, with decorated medallions.

Group of Tall Cylindrical Vases ; medallions with powder-blue *soufflé* field; decorations in polychrome. Khang-he period, A.D. 1661–1722. (From the Andrews collection, London.)

Group of small **Double-gourd-shaped** Bottles.

Ovoid Vase, and **Plaque** ; powder-blue *soufflé;* floral medallions.

Large Plaque. Sky-blue *soufflé* ground; medallions with the dog Fo, phoenixes, etc. Khang-he period.

Pair of Large Bowls, on the lower tier. Interior, white ground, with decoration. Exterior, scallop-shaped panels formed with polychrome, in transparent green glaze, alternating with others of brilliant red and floral subjects. Khang-he period, A.D. 1661–1722.

Two Small Jars, with covers; decorated medallions with white ground.

Large Beaker ; decoration like the last.

On the end shelves :

Two Large Ovoid Jars, with covers; *soufflé* blue, with floral medallions, birds, etc., of exceptional quality as respects paste and painting. Khang-he period.

Two Double-Gourd-Shaped Bottles ; blue *soufflé*; polychrome medallions.

Two Ovoid Vases ; deep *soufflé* ground; medallions. Khang-he period.

Ewer. Sky-blue, with medallions, and Louis XV. mounting.

A series of teapots, plates and bottles with medallions on sky-blue ground, is also worthy of note on this side. (Principally from European and Eastern collections.)

EGG-SHELL PLATES, CUPS AND SAUCERS.

This portion of the collection occupies five cases along the gallery side.

These fragile specimens are made from "hard paste" porcelain with wonderful skill; of materials the purest, and

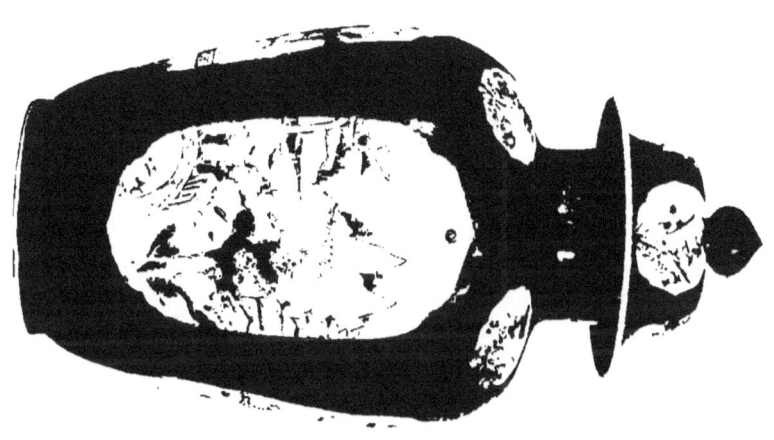

CASE 6.

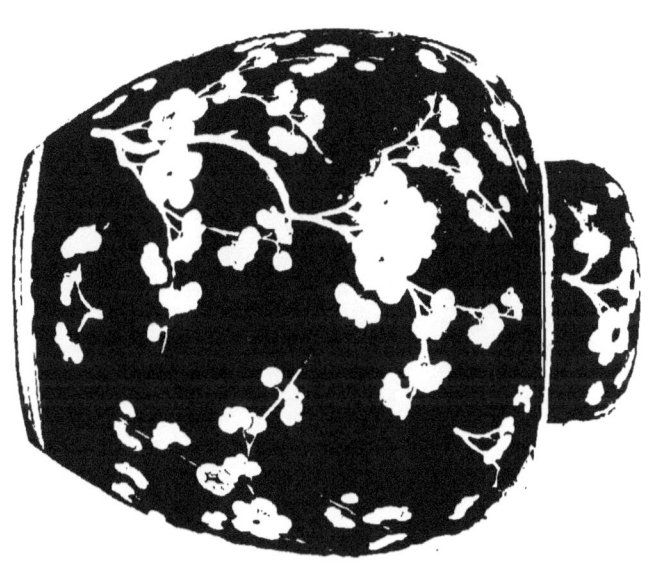

CASE 9.

most carefully prepared and manipulated through every stage, from the wet clay to the baking and the final painting and firing. The subjects selected for the decoration are very numerous, including landscapes, interiors, figures, fruit, flowers, birds, butterflies, animals, etc.; painted in various colors, often relieved with gilding, over the glaze, on the white ground, showing the texture and quality of the paste. The central subjects are generally inclosed in from one to seven borders, carefully wrought with intricate geometrical tracery or fretted designs, with vignettes or small panels left for separate embellishment.

The so-called "rose-back" plates properly rank first in this class. They are thus styled from the border on the under side, enameled in rose-color, usually solid *soufflé;* and are valued according to the quality of the tone.

CASE 7.

In this case are twenty-one "rose-back" and other plates, with two and three borders, enclosing a central subject; also delicate egg-shell cups and saucers; all decorated with enamel colors and gilding over the glaze—in which predominate the half-tones and the carmine or rose derived from chloride of gold. Yung-tching period, A.D. 1723–1735. (Many of the plates are from the Magniac, Wells, and Essex collections.)

The upper shelf contains **one of a pair of hexagonal lanterns,** of egg-shell porcelain, with reticulated panels, each with a circular medallion decorated with figures, delicately painted in light colors, and surrounded by borders. Yung-tching period, A.D. 1723–1735. (Another is seen in Case 11.)

CASE 8.

Twenty-one rose-back and other egg-shell plates, with three and four borders; and eight delicate egg-shell cups and saucers; all decorated in enamel colors and gilding over the glaze; half-tones and rose-tint predominating. Yung-tching period, A.D. 1723–1735.

In this case also is **one of a pair of hexagonal egg-shell lanterns**, with ovoid body and perforated angular neck. The panels are embellished with figures, landscapes and interiors. The decorative subject appears to be a historical event. It is very skillfully rendered, in very clear and lustrous colors. Khang-he period, A.D. 1661–1722. (From the Mary J. Morgan collection. The other one of the pair is in Case 10.)

CASE 9.

This case contains nine masterpieces of egg-shell porcelain, in the shape of

Nine Seven-bordered Rose-back Plates. The design consists of seven delicately drawn borders, forming a frame to the central panel; the latter with figures—generally court ladies and children in rich attire, with various accessories—deftly painted on a white ground of fine texture, in from seven to ten colors, with gilding; and fired with wonderful accuracy. Yung-tching period, A.D. 1723–1735.

The four blue " **hawthorn** " jars shown in this case, and which properly belong to the blue and white series, are among the rarest existing; produced in the XVII. century, but unrivaled to-day. The paste is hard and of purest texture, well suited to the unusually deep and vivid cobalt blue. One jar has the original cover. Khang-he period. (Each of these jars has filled its place in former collections. Among them is the celebrated one from the Blenheim collection, which is considered the gem, but it has not the original cover.)

Four Egg-shell Plates, with two borders; on the lower shelf.

Large Egg-shell Lantern; ovoid hexagonal, with circular medallions containing carefully painted figures and landscapes. Yung-tching period, A.D. 1723–1735. (From the Wells collection, London.)

In this case are also

RICE-GRAIN PIECES WITH PIERCED
ORNAMENTATION.

This beautiful decoration is made by piercing or cutting out the designs in the body of the porcelain, and filling in the apertures with glaze, leaving them semi-transparent. This is a work of considerable skill. The design is sometimes a dragon, sometimes leaves or flowers, but oftener a fret or star diaper. Noteworthy are:

Globular Vase, a flawless example of the variety. Pure quality and egg-shell texture. Kien-long (Chien-lung) period, A.D. 1736–1795.

The other six (small) specimens, pierced and reticulated, are of the Khang-he period.

CASE 10.

This case contains twenty-two rose-back *soufflé* and other egg-shell plates, some of which have five borders; with eight delicate egg-shell cups and saucers; painted with enamel colors and gilding over the glaze. In the coloring half-tones predominate, together with the carmine or rose of the Yung-tching period, A.D. 1723–1735. Among the rose-back plates on the upper shelf is a unique example with an engraved fret design on the *soufflé* rose back.

On the upper shelf is one of a pair of **egg-shell lanterns,** ovoid-hexagonal, and perforated angular neck. The decoration is a figure subject with landscapes and interiors, in translucent enamels, illustrating the highest point of this branch of Chinese art. Khang-he period, A.D. 1661–1722. (The companion piece is in Case 8. These pieces have figured in notable collections in China and Europe. They were obtained at the sale of the collection of Mrs. Mary J. Morgan in New York.)

CASE 11.

In this case are grouped twenty-one rose-back *soufflé* and other egg-shell plates with four, five and six borders; with eight delicate egg-shell cups and saucers; decorated in

enamel colors over the glaze. The carmine and rose tones
are predominant. (A number of these objects are from the
Essex, Wells, and other noted collections.)

On the upper shelf is one of a pair of **hexagonal lanterns**,
egg-shell; reticulated panels within fret borders, each enclosing a circular medallion with delicately painted figures
and other objects. (The companion piece is in Case 7.)
Yung-tching period, A.D. 1723–1735.

The following thirteen cases are along the wall and in the
niches of the gallery.

CASE 12.

This case contains twenty-two specimens of hard paste,
painted over the glaze in polychrome, in which the coral
red, from oxide of iron, predominates. This color is brilliant, but not translucent like the other enamels, and produces a striking contrast. The addition of this color has
given to objects of the sort a rank among the most noted
productions of the Khang-he period, A.D. 1661–1722. A few
pieces show the green enamel predominant.

Noteworthy in this case are:

Three Cylindrical Vases, and **two beakers** with spreading base and top. A red, conventional, floral design over-
spreads the body, with medallions and borders, in which
the green predominates. (The beakers are from the Leyland collection.)

Tall Ovoid Vase, with superbly painted medallions enclosing figures and other objects. Silver top.

Cylindrical Vase ; polychrome border at base and neck;
white ground, with dragons and fish in red, about the body
and upper part of the neck. Khang-he period.

Two Small Cylindrical Vases ; about the body, green
and red bands of archaic design.

Large Spherical Bottle ; decorated in red with the symbolic carp; about the neck a delicate sprig with blossoms.
Khang-he period, A.D. 1661–1722.

Two Water-Jars; hexagonal, with handles; floral design,
the red predominant. Khang-he period.

CASE 9.

CASE 10.

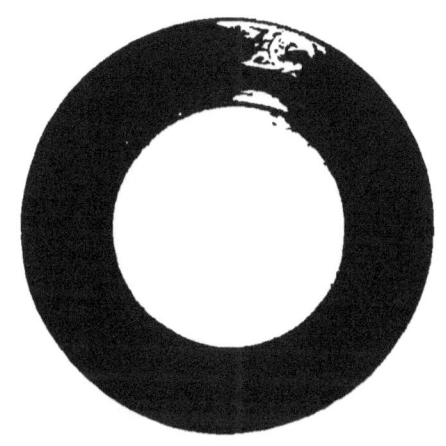

CASE 12.

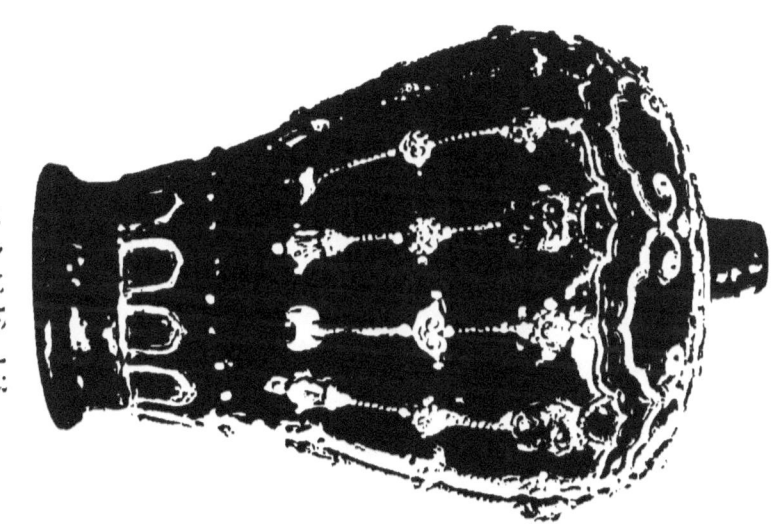

CASE 13.

Two Small Bottles ; gourd shape ; with polychrome decoration.

Beaker-Shaped Vase ; decorated in polychrome ; the green predominant. Khang-he period.

Square Vase; figures of divinities in bold relief, in various colors on a white ground. Khang-he period.

CASE 13.

Primitive pieces, ascribed to provinces of China where porcelain manufacture has long been forgotten. The biscuit, which shows here and there through the glaze, has less kaolin than the later porcelain, and is of a fine sandy grain, dense and heavy. The decorations are modeled in low relief; the enamel colors are mainly lapis-lazuli blue, shading into purple or violet, often resembling the color of the wild apple or plum skin, amber yellow and turquoise blue ; the interior generally glazed with green. Among the monochrome objects in this case are several of the *clair de lune* variety.

The colors and shapes of those early periods are here fairly well represented. Of the fifteen pieces in this case, some are of the Sung dynasty, A. D. 960–1260; some of the Yuan dynasty, A. D. 1260–1368; and others probably of the earlier Ming periods.

In the centre is a large, well-modeled figure of Kwan-yin, a Boddisttva, with a child and a parrot. The figure is seated under a canopy formed of a cave of rocks, with Buddhistic symbols. The folds of the robe are in light turquoise enamel; the parrot glazed with lustrous, transparent green.

Of the jars:

Oviform Jar, with cover; reticulated outer surface, with symbolic designs and figures of legendary beings, modeled in low relief on the clay, and enameled mainly in turquoise. Yuan dynasty.

Second Jar, with cover; light turquoise glaze, with low relief in other colors, representing the Pa-sien figures and their symbols. Yuan dynasty.

Third Jar; glazed in lapis-lazuli blue; with a design of figures similar to the first, representing the criticism of various accomplishments, modeled in low relief. Yuan dynasty.

Fourth Jar; smaller; floral relief picked out in various glazes on a lapis-lazuli ground.

Two Smaller Jars; aquatic plants modeled in low relief, glazed in turquoise and green; purple ground.

Large Vase, broad feeding-bottle shape; about the body, boldly modeled symbols in relief, arranged in bands and festoons upheld by curious masks. Border of archaic design at base. Yuan dynasty.

Another Tall Vase, of shape like the last; aquatic plants in low relief, glazed in colors; lapis-lazuli ground. Yuan dynasty.

Bowl, *clair de lune* (moonlight) glaze. Sung dynasty.

Coupe, *clair de lune* glaze shading into purplish. Sung dynasty.

Bottle-shaped Vase; dark purple glazed ground; openwork borders in turquoise blue enamel. Ming period.

Small Vase, low; *clair de lune* glaze.

Two Garden Seats, glazed in deep lapis-lazuli blue; band of raised buttons about a band of openwork in turquoise glaze, with representations of the dog Fo in purple.

CASE 14.

Cabinet specimens of small dimensions; principally of the Ming dynasty, during the XV. and XVI. centuries. Several of the objects show unglazed portions of the biscuit—a paste with less kaolin, and characteristic of the early Mings. For the painting, five colors seem usually to suffice; applied on the biscuit or white glaze. The case contains eighty-two objects; among them, grotesque figures and animals, vases, sacrificial cups, and small ornaments; all in rich iridescent polychrome, the green predominant.

Among the more interesting objects are:

Figure of Pon-tai, a Buddhistic demigod, modeled in

CASE 13.

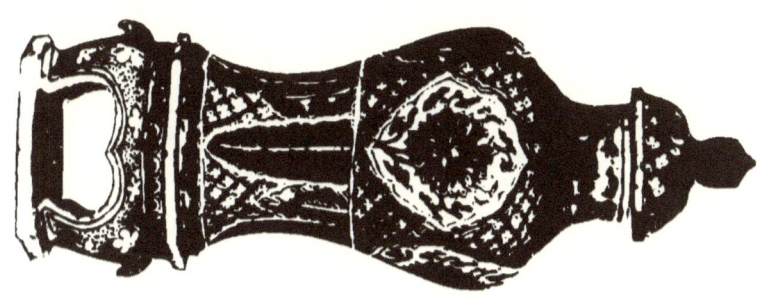

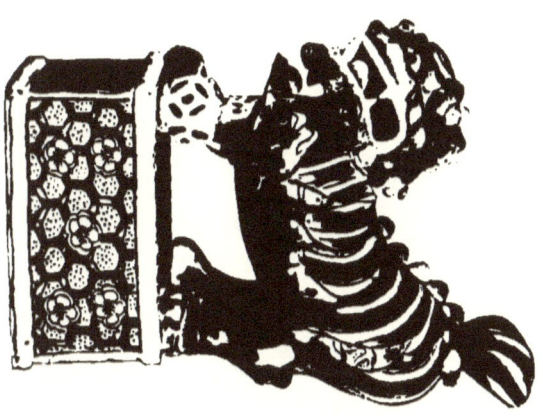

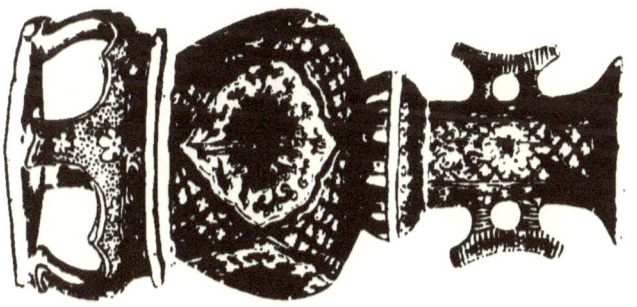

CASE 14.

unglazed biscuit, except the harlequin robe, which is glazed in polychrome enamels.

Figure of Kowan-te, a popular chivalrous character of Chinese mythology; on a raised seat with back.

Figure of a Chinese Lady, standing, holding a fan; robes in polychrome. Ming period.

Pair of Figurines, mounted on the dog Fo; in various glazes. Ming period.

Open Work Cages, for birds and insects, in biscuit, decorated with various glazes. Ming period.

Five Small Vases, polychrome. Ming dynasty. (From the Blenheim collection.)

Libation or Sacrificial Cups; various decorations. Ming dynasty.

Pair of Bowls; reticulated outer surface; polychrome decoration of the Ming type. Date-mark, Khang-he. (A.D. 1661-1722.)

Unique Pipe; decorated in various glazes.

Large Libation-Cup; called also **Marriage Cup;** without base; surrounded by free dragons that form decorated handles, in various glazes.

Tablet; biscuit porcelain; decorated in various colors. carved teak wood stand. Ming dynasty.

Series of Wine-Cups, in various shapes; some resembling flowers and fruit; glazed in transparent colors. Ming period.

Small objects, with landscapes, etc.

CASE 15.

Teapots, of various types and periods; with bowls, cups and other cabinet objects of the XVI., XVII. and XVIII. centuries; with polychrome decorations over the glaze. Sixty pieces; among them, specimens with a transparent lustrous green of the Ming and Khang-he periods; others with the rose-color of the Yung-tching period.

Teapot; in form of a vase supported by the dog Fo; polychrome decoration.

Teapot; lotus form; rose petals; green seeds; dragon stem handles.

Two Teapots ; raised medallions; decoration chiefly rose and green; spout and handle, the dog Fo.

Sugar-bowl ; openwork body in polychrome ; handle glazed in yellow with black stripes.

Teapot; polychrome; rose and black medallions.

Another ; similar form and decoration.

Teapot; hexagonal; openwork medallion; rose-color predominant.

Teapot; ball-shaped ; medallions on diapered green ground.

Teapot; square; medallions with poultry and butterflies.

Large Flat Teapot ; round; polychrome borders; circular *show* mark in red and gold on a white ground.

Sugar-bowl ; handle; outer surface, openwork decorated in various colors.

Set: European design; teapot, cream-jug, sugar-bowl, cups and saucers. Figure subject on black ground.

Tall Ewer, Persian shape; polychrome, with the mark *show* on the cover in red; surmounted by the dog Fo.

Teapot ; openwork; yellow and green ground.

Teapot ; similar to the last.

Teapot ; monkey form.

Teapot ; form of a cock; glazes chiefly green, yellow and purple.

Teapot ; form of a fish; white, green and purple.

Another ; similar in form and decoration.

Teapot ; raised panels, on black ground.

Teapot ; raised panels; polychrome decoration on black ground.

Teapot; form of lotus flower; natural colors.

Teapot; turquoise glaze; raised medallions.

Teapot; poultry medallions.

Teapot; form of lotus receptacle, with seed; glazed in yellow and green.

Teapot; figure mounted on a dragon; glazed in various colors.

CASE 15.

Two Teapots; cylinder formed of bamboo-stems; joined in yellow, green and lilac glaze.
Teapot; ovoid; bamboo; color like the last.
Bowl, with handle; open work; flower decoration on a stippled ground.
Two Teapots, peach-shaped; green and yellow.

In Cases 16, 17, 18, 19, are grouped types of hard and soft paste porcelain painted in blue; principally cobalt blue of various shades and depths, representing the XV., XVI. and XVII. centuries, beginning with the Seuen-ti period under the Mings (A.D. 1426-1436), and ending with the Khang-he period (A.D. 1661-1722).

The blue, as already mentioned, is painted on the paste before the glazing is applied; and its brilliant appearance is due to the firing. The paste is very absorbent after the first baking, or before glazing, and it is difficult, accordingly, to make the blue lines clear and sharp. Among the clever expedients used to overcome this difficulty is the application of a gum before painting the design. Blue and white porcelain has long been esteemed in Europe, where it has furnished many models for the potters, as at Delft, etc.

CASE 16.

Seventy Cabinet objects. Among the hard paste and the larger objects, the following should be noted:
Large Ovoid Jar; butterflies and flowers, in white reserve on a deep blue ground; medallions, with flowers and other objects. Khang-he period.
Two Small Trumpet-shaped Vases, with covers; floral medallions, with figures. Khang-he period.
Two Tall Vases, cylindrical; floral design with conventional dragons, in white reserve on blue ground. Khang-he period.
Jar; flower-bouquets; including the lotus and peony in arabesque setting. Khang-he period.

44566

Tall Vase; spherical body and long neck; conventional tiger lily. Khang-he period.

Pair of Vases, cylindrical; decorated with several distinct borders; a white ground with blue tracery alternating with a band on blue ground; white dragons in reserve.

Bottles; fine hard paste; lace design in blue.

Pair of Double Bottles; blue tracery; figures, among other small objects.

Small Pear-shaped Bottle; soft paste of creamy white; decoration, delicate blue, dragons, conventional clouds, and sprays of water.

Another Bottle, similar in form and decoration. Raised base.

Pair of Covered Bowls; soft paste; delicate tracery in blue. Scuen-ti period of the Mings.

Pair of Small Covered Cups; soft paste; light tracery in blue. Same period.

Round Coupe; soft paste; butterfly decoration in deep cobalt blue. Ming period.

Several Small Bottles; soft paste; lace-pattern tracery in blue.

Two Small Teapots; conventional blue.

Pear-shaped Bottle; hard paste; deep blue, with medallions, etc., on fine white ground.

Two Teapots, Persian shape; deep blue arabesque and diaper.

CASE 17.

Seventy pieces, blue under the glaze. The following specimens may be noticed:

Tall Vase, beaker form; historical subject; blue on white ground. Khang-he period, A.D. 1661–1722.

Two Cylindrical Vases; lustrous blue; peonies and foliage in reserve; scalloped border about the shoulders and base. Khang-he period, A.D. 1661–1722. (From the Orrock collection.)

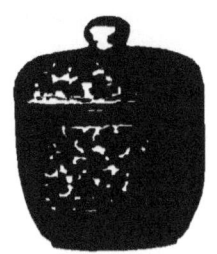

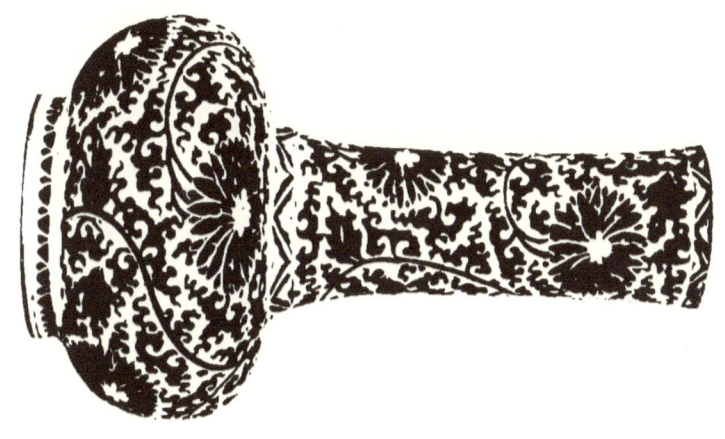

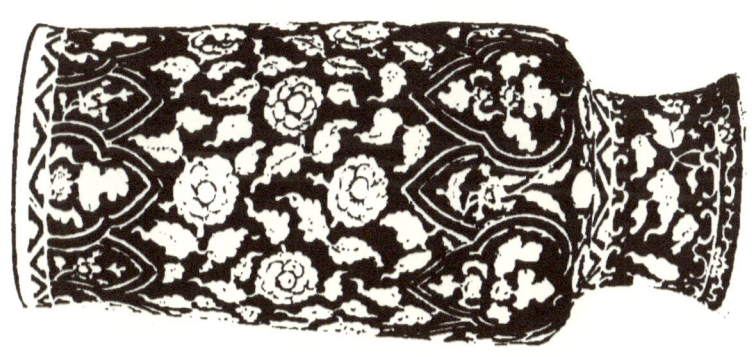

Three Vases ; globular body, long neck; decorated with deep blue conventional tiger-lily design over the whole surface. Khang-he period, A.D. 1661-1722.

Large Ovoid Jar, with cover; medallion design in cobalt blue, on a white body color. Same period.

Three Small Vases, cylindrical; series of borders, varying from a translucent blue ground with dragons in white reserve, to others decorated in blue on the white body color. Khang-he period.

Small Bottle, pear shaped; deep blue, with medallions on the white body color.

Vase, baluster-shaped; soft paste; deep blue arabesque designs.

Pair of Small Bottles ; spherical body, slender neck; blue arabesques of fruit and flowers.

Three Small Jars ; blue, with medallions, etc., on white ground.

Square Vase ; soft paste; delicate blue flower and arabesque designs, on creamy white ground.

Groups of Small Bottles and Vases, all in blue tracery.

CASE 18.

Sixty-four pieces, blue under the glaze; including specimens of the XVII. and XVIII. centuries. Note especially:

Five Pieces in the central portion of the upper shelf; viz., two tall vases, two tall jars with covers, and one beaker-shaped vase. The decoration is on slightly raised panels, about the body; with flowers and figures in blue.

On the lower shelves are to be observed:

Two Tall Vases, trumpet shaped, with wide base; elongated white panels with landscapes and floral designs, reserved from the beaded cobalt blue, with white raised butterflies and flowers.

Vase ; ovoid ; similar decoration.

Small Vase, ovoid ; soft paste ; cream-white medallions with impressed blue floral designs, and butterflies.

Pear-shaped Vase; blue; medallions and lace-pattern borders.

Pair of Jars; handles painted in blue medallion design, with tracery. Khang-he period.

Pair of Bottles; dragons in blue.

Small Bottle, pear-shaped; blue tracery.

Small Jar; dragons and blue tracery. Khang-he period.

Pair of Gourd-shaped Vases; figure subjects. Silver top.

Pair of Teapots, Persian shape; blue decoration.

Pair of Small Bottles; spherical body; blue lace-pattern; borders and floral medallions.

Small Teapot, globular; blue arabesque, with small figures in white reserve.

Sundry small bottles and vases.

CASE 19.

Fifty-four pieces decorated in blue under the glaze; including specimens of the XVII. and XVIII. centuries, as follows:

Large Ovoid Jar, with cover; hard paste; court personages; deep cobalt blue. Khang-he period, A.D. 1661–1722. (From the Leyland collection.)

Pair of Tall Vases, trumpet shape, with spreading base. Conventional peonies and lilies, uniformly overspreading a white ground of exceptional quality. Khang-he period.

Large Bottle; cobalt blue; the pavilion of a divinity surrounded by water with dragons, on a fine white paste. Khang-he period.

Two Tall Vases; panels enclosing figures and flowers.

Teapot, Persian shape; openwork outer surface in white; deep blue tracery.

Ovoid Jar; landscape and floral medallions.

Large Cups; flower decoration; white interior.

Sundry small Vases and Bottles, blue.

The four cases following conclude the series with polychrome over the glaze, of the XVII. and XVIII. centuries.

CASE 17 (Lower).　　　CASE 20 (Upper).

CASE 10

CASE 20.

Thirty-eight pieces; among them egg-shell porcelains with elaborate embellishments; including specimens, of the XVIII. century, styled by Jacquemart "Mandarin Vases."

Two Tall Vases, egg-shell; square, with handles, and covers surmounted by the dog Fo. Ground-color, rose with arabesque diaper; the large panels with mandarin figures and various objects, in polychrome. (From the Andrews collection, London.)

Pair of Vases, ovoid; white ground with mandarin figures and other objects, in polychrome on a coral and gold fretted ground.

Pair of Vases, ovoid; white ground; mandarin figures in polychrome enamels.

Pair of Egg-shell Vases; figure subject in polychrome; the rose predominating. Yung-tching period, A.D. 1723–1735.

Small Egg-shell Vase; arabesque design in blue and gold; two white medallions with European figure subject, in polychrome.

Egg-shell Plate; Taoist divinity, with a stag, painted on white ground.

Two Egg-shell Plates; horses, etc., in polychrome.

Plate; openwork border; figure subject in polychrome.

Plate; European figure subject, in polychrome. Khienlong period, A.D. 1736–1795.

Among the specimens of the Khang-he period are:

Tall Vase, beaker-shaped; archaic design in polychrome, chiefly green enamel.

Vase, beaker-shaped; landscape medallions in polychrome; white circular reserve, with red fish.

Large Plate, semi-egg-shell, hung on the wall; Chinese princess in rich robes, with a child, in polychrome on white ground; about them a fungus-formed border, with butterflies, etc., on a stippled green ground. The outer border has a conventional design in red.

Pitong Vase; openwork bamboo and modeled foliage, glazed in turquoise.

Two Reticulated Hanging Vases; form as if made of twisted and knotted cords, in various colors; held by bands and borders.

Small Vases, in shape of fruits; céladon glaze, with light green enamel foliage.

Sacrificial or Marriage Cup; dragons and arabesques in delicate colors.

Jar, with cover; floral decoration, in natural colors, over the whole surface. XVIII. century.

Egg-Shell Cups and Saucers, with delicate decoration.

CASE 21.

Twelve specimens, of the XVII. and XVIII. centuries, mostly of large proportions; decorated in polychrome over the glaze.

Large Jardiniere, nearly globular; boldly drawn design; dragons in various colors, amid conventional waves and spray; with gilding. Khang-he period. (From the Marquis collection, Paris.)

Pair of Tall Vases, with gilt-bronze mounting; slender and graceful form; inverted sections over which are panels of various shapes, with figures, chimaeras, flowers and other objects, about which is an arabesque design chiefly of lustrous green; the other colors spreading over the fine white body. Khang-he period, A.D. 1661–1722.

Large Plaque; elaborate polychrome decoration—a terrace, horses, and other objects, on a white ground; outer border of floral design, chiefly in red. Khang-he period, A.D. 1661–1722.

Large Plaque, companion to the preceding; flowers and a basket, in delicate natural colors, on a fine white ground; about them a medallion border with *ky-lins*, birds, and other objects, in transparent polychrome enamels. Khang-he period.

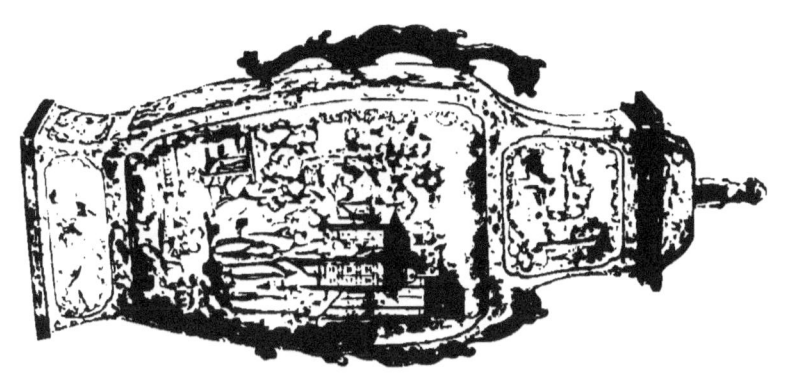

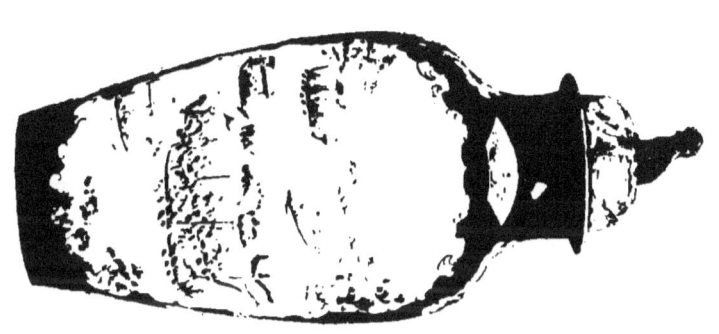

CASE 20.

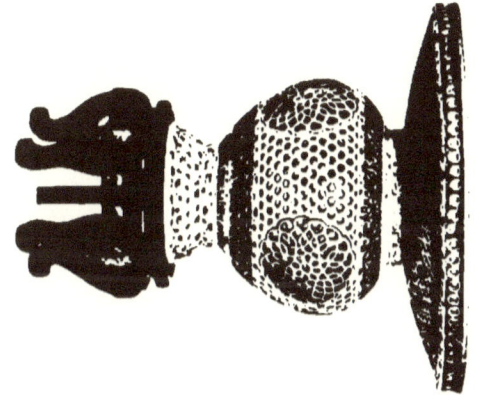

CASE 23.

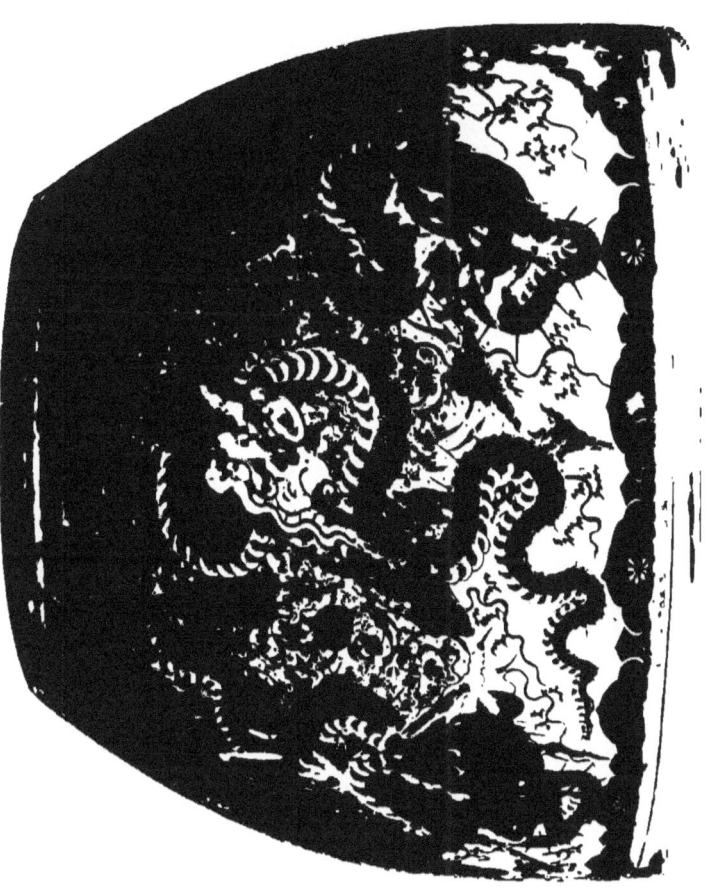

CASE 21.

Pair of Large Plaques; in centre, phoenixes, with flowers, in natural-color enamels. In the outer borders, animals in medallions, with arabesque tracery in red and gold. Yung-tching period, A.D. 1723–1735.

Large Jar, with cover; floral medallions, etc., in delicately colored enamels, the light rose tint predominant. Yung-tching period, A.D. 1723–1735.

Egg-Shell Plate; figure riding on a *ky-lin*, accompanied by a boy with a sword and a scroll, on a white ground.

Egg-Shell Plate; bird perched on a twig with peach blossoms, on a fine white ground.

Another Plate; figure subject, on a white ground.

Unglazed Rouge-Box; white paste; dragon in free relief.

CASE 22.

Eleven great specimens, of types similar to those of Case 21; decorated in polychrome over the glaze.

Large Jar, with cover; enameled black ground, with green arabesque foliage and rose-colored chrysanthemums; leaf-shaped medallions in white reserve, with flowers, birds and animals, in delicate natural colors. Neck and base encircled by fret borders in light tints. Yung-tching period, A.D. 1723–1735. (Companion in Case 3.)

Two Large Plaques, on upper shelf. In centre, flowers and birds, on a white ground; about them scallop-formed panels on green ground, with landscapes, flowers and other objects, with arabesques in red; in the smaller outer border, white reserve vignettes, with horses, birds, etc. Khang-he period, A.D. 1661–1722.

Large Plaque, semi-egg-shell; centre with a dramatic figure subject in brilliant colors. Border of figures and flowers, the delicate rose-tint predominant. Yung-tching period, A.D. 1723–1735.

Another Plaque, with figures in a garden; in outer border, small figures and horses in various attitudes. This piece shows the transition from the green to the carmine style of decoration. Khang-he period, A.D. 1661–1723.

Two Beakers, octagonal; decoration in polychrome. Yung-tching period. (Companions to the jars shown in case 23.)

Large Jar; with Taoist symbols in green and yellow, on a purple ground of the Khang-he period.

Two Pear-shaped Bottles; red decoration, and arabesque design of the Khien-long period, A.D. 1736–1795.

CASE 23.

Fourteen pieces of the XVII. and XVIII. centuries; similar in decoration to those of Cases 21 and 22. Among them, the following are to be noticed :

Large Jar, ovoid, with cover; polychrome floral design, with peonies, birds, etc. ; in seven transparent colors, the green and red of the early Khang-he period predominant.

Two Beakers; polychrome flowers and birds, similar to the last. Same period.

Tall Vase, cylindrical; figure subject in translucent cobalt blue on white ground; with red and green representations of immortals. Border about the neck with the characteristic *show*. Khang-he period. (Arkwright collection.)

Tall Vase, cylindrical; polychrome; white medallions with flowers, within green ground. Khang-he period.

Two Vases, cylindrical; bronze mounting; polychrome; red (of iron) predominant in conventional floral designs, with scallop-band in other enamels. Khang-he period, A.D. 1661–1772.

Vase, of like form, coloring and decoration, without the mounting. Same period.

Large Plaque; various figures, and pavilions, in translucent enamels. Same period.

Pair of Reticulated Vases; decorated in various tints. Yung-tching period. (From the Arkwright collection.)

Vase, ovoid, floral decoration in polychrome on black ground.

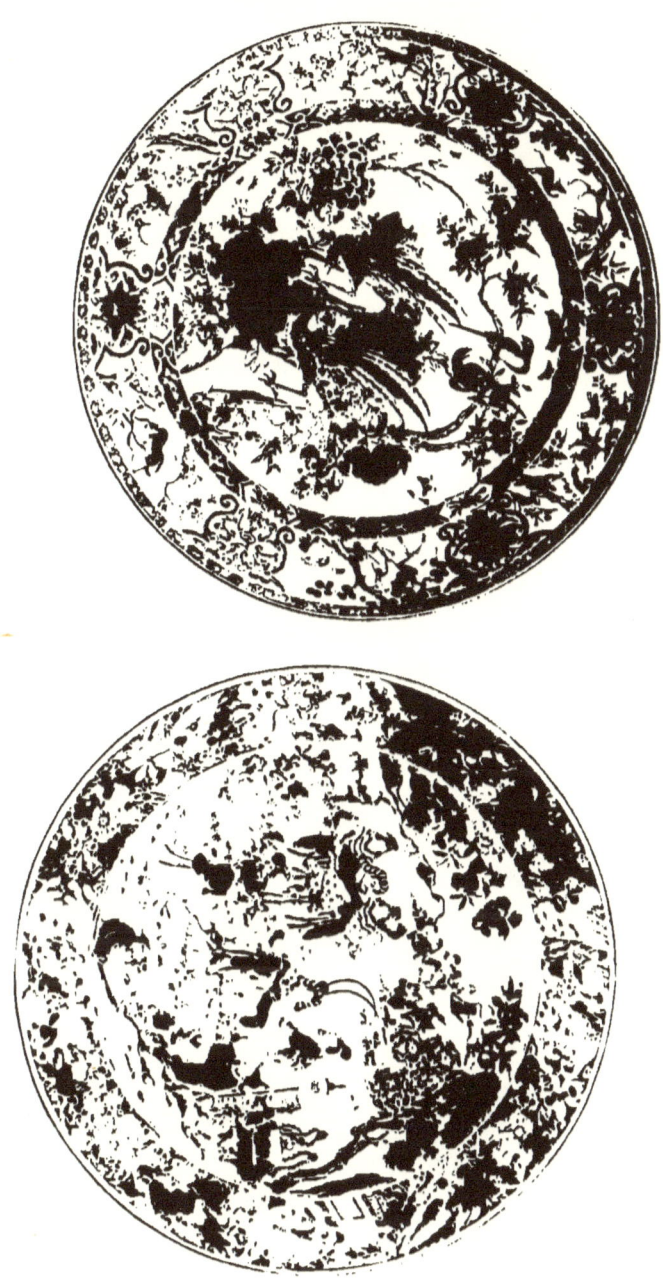

CASE 28.

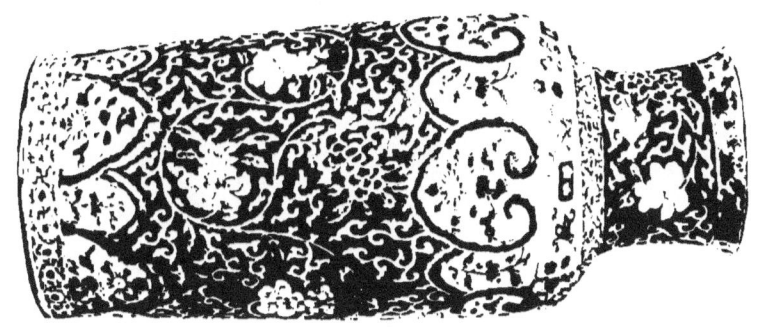

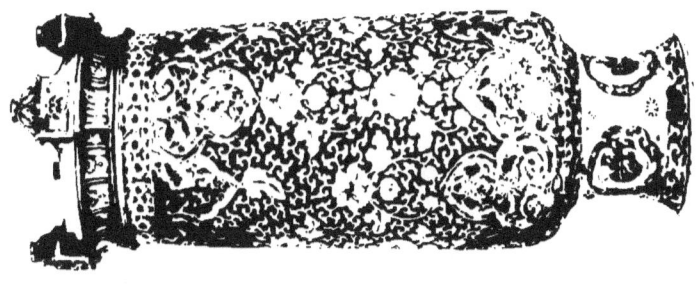

CASE 22.

www.ingramcontent.com/pod-product-compliance
Lightning Source LLC
Chambersburg PA
CBHW020758020726
47495CB00008B/2487